CW00471626

BONDED TO THE ALIEN CENTURION

WARRIORS OF THE LATHAR

MINA CARTER

NEW YORK TIMES & USA TODAY BESTSELLING AUTHOR

Copyright © 2018 by Mina Carter

All rights reserved.

No part of this book may be reproduced in any form or by any electronic or mechanical means, including information storage and retrieval systems, without written permission from the author, except for the use of brief quotations in a book review.

CONTENTS

1

"*T*ell me about these human females."

Holy *draanth*. He was in the same room as the emperor himself. Sardaan K'Vass blinked and resisted the temptation to pinch himself. Standing as he was just behind his commander, Fenriis, no one would notice if he did but that wasn't the point. He was a warrior with a headful of braids. He had a reputation to uphold. Still, he couldn't help the awe washing through him as he looked around the room. It was filled to the brim with legends.

Warriors from the other vessels crowded the room, all facing one way. Emperor Daaynal K'Saan stood there next to his sister-sons, War Commander

Tarrick and Lord Healer Laarn, his grim face and scarred body a sight to behold. On the other side of the emperor was his champion, Xaandril, one arm in a sling, and, surprisingly, a human female.

Sardaan watched her from the corner of his eye. Dressed in a curious mixture of warrior's leathers and human attire, she seemed to be with Xaandril himself. That in itself was a surprise. The big, gruff champion was not known to frequent the pleasure houses and the story of how he'd lost his mate and child, and his reaction, was the stuff of legend.

Yet, he appeared protective and possessive about the little human female, glaring at any male who looked at her for too long. It was an unspoken challenge that the woman was his. If he hadn't claimed her yet, it wouldn't be long. Sardaan certainly wouldn't take him on. Even though the champion was recovering from injury, it would still be suicide.

"We have the human vice president, Madison Cole, onboard," Fenriis said, his deep voice filling the briefing room. "There seems to be some political issues. The human male, Hopkins, seems to have orders from above her, from the president himself, indicating promises she makes will not be honored."

Daaynal frowned, a deep crease between his

brows. His braids, more than Sardaan had ever seen on a warrior, brushed his shoulder as he looked at Fenriis. "You think she intends to play us for fools?"

Danaar, next to Fenriis, rumbled in the back of his throat, but the commander lifted a hand slightly to silence his second in command. Sardaan watched the interplay with interest. Danaar's feelings toward the human female were no secret. Hadn't been since the moment she'd stepped aboard their ship.

"Unsure. I do think she's being cut out of their command structure. Hopkins spouted off something about reprisals when she returns home because of her stance toward us."

There was another grumble from Danaar but he didn't speak. Like Sardaan, he knew better than to interrupt such males in conversation. But Sardaan didn't miss the tiny flicker of the emperor's gaze toward the big warrior. Shit. If Daaynal took offense...

"Her stance toward us?" the emperor continued, his attention once again on Fenriis. "A good one, I take it?"

Fenriis nodded. "Seems level-headed and open to both negotiation and the possibility of integration of our two species."

"One species," the Lord Healer interrupted.

"Humans are a subspecies of Lathar. They literally are us. But smaller."

"And we still have women," the woman at Xaandril's side interrupted, something that made more than a few males around the room frown. But neither the emperor nor the lord healer seemed annoyed, instead nodding in agreement as the woman spoke.

"Madison Cole is a good woman," she continued. "Fair and level with good policies. She's always fought for the people, even against overwhelming odds, and it doesn't surprise me that she's being reasonable about human-Lathar negotiations. *Nor* does it surprise me," she stressed quickly, "that the asshats in Terra-command are moving against her. They've been trying to discredit her for years. She's good people."

Sardaan watched her openly now, along with most of the room. Daaynal smiled. "Gentlemen, please let me introduce Kenna Reynolds, one of our delightful Terran guests. She has been most gracious in aiding our understanding of her people."

Sardaan easily decoded the emperor's words. The woman had to be one of the women taken from the first Terran base the Lathar had discovered.

Stories had been going around about them since their discovery. They were all supposed to be military women. Now, having seen her and others on the human ship just off their port bow, he finally understood what that meant.

Kenna lifted her chin, looking around the room with a slight smile on her lips as she nodded in acknowledgment. "Gentlemen."

"So... you think dealing with the vice president will get us nowhere?" the emperor demanded of the human female, who shrugged.

"Without knowing more about the situation and speaking to her, I can't say that. I've been out of the loop for a while."

She flashed a grin at Xaandril, and Sardaan was surprised to see the slight softening of his features as he looked at the tiny female. Yeah, the champion had it bad. Why hadn't he claimed her yet? She was right there, and much smaller than the champion. There was no way she'd be able to win in a challenge fight.

"Who else are we dealing with?" Daaynal transferred his attention back to Fenriis. To his credit, the war commander didn't even flinch in the face of the emperor's harsh manner, but Sardaan hadn't expected anything else. They were all K'Vass, the best warrior clan out there.

"The human ship *TSS Defiant* originally arrived commanded by a General Hopkins, but after his attempted attack on us, command transferred to a Major General Black. Female. I can't tell how old she is, I..." Fenriis shrugged a little. "My exposure to females has been limited. If I were to guess, I would say she's a warrior in her prime."

The image of the beautiful Terran woman formed instantly in Sardaan's mind when Fenriis mentioned her name, and he kept his expression level only with hard-fought control. As communications officer, he'd been the first to speak to her and had been instantly captivated. She was tiny and beautiful... her direct gaze affected him on levels he'd never experienced before, and he instantly wanted more. He'd kill to get her into a challenge circle and claim her.

"Wait..." Kenna butted in, her expression rapt. "Did you say Major General *Black?*"

Fenriis nodded, the males around the table looking at the human female. She certainly had all of Sardaan's attention. Any information he could glean on Black was good. If he ever managed to meet her, he wanted as much intel as possible to further his interests.

"You know this name?" Daaynal asked.

Kenna whistled, and nodded. "Oh yeah... I know Black. *Everyone* in the service knows Black."

"Explain." The emperor's demand was brusque and would have made a lesser warrior quake in their boots but Kenna's lips merely quirked.

"Black is a legend in her own lifetime. Like a seriously scary lady. Been in just about every conflict...like ever. Totally badass."

His human female was a warrior like him.

Sardaan couldn't help the small grin that passed over his lips. *Badass.* Even he could work out the human word was a good one. Black would make a worthy mate indeed... once he got near enough to claim her. He cast a quick glance at the males around the table. Half looked as interested in information on Black as he was. *Draanth,* he'd probably have to fight for the chance to claim her.

He gritted his teeth as determination filled him. He would do whatever he had to. She was *his.* It would be good to have a mate, someone to share his life with. She would soon adapt to life on board a Latharian vessel.

"Good. Then we need her on-side, preferably

mated to one of our warriors," Daaynal announced, looking at Fenriis.

For a moment Sardaan's heart almost stopped in his chest, but then he remembered that Fenriis already had a mate, the lovely Lady Amanda. "Commander, you are the only one of us who has actually spoken to the female in question at length. Opinion?"

"She's a capable warrior and in my opinion, nobody's fool. She will not be easily manipulated. However, during the conversation I had with her earlier, she did betray interest, a very small interest, in one of our warriors."

Sardaan blinked, replaying the conversation in his mind as he tried to figure out who Fenriis was talking about—and, more importantly, who he'd have to kill to get a shot at the female he wanted—but came up blank.

There had been interference on the line during the communication, so he'd had to pay attention to his systems to keep it cleaned up. He'd taken his attention off the screen a couple of times.

"Who?" the emperor demanded.

Fenriis turned to the side slightly, leaving Sardaan himself in the spotlight. He half turned before he realized there was no one behind him.

"Me?" His voice betrayed his surprise, and then pleasure flooded his system. Black had shown interest in *him?* Perhaps this would be easier than he'd thought.

"Yes, you. Your Highness, this is Sardaan K'Vass, a kinsman of mine." Fenriis gave a small smile as he urged Sardaan to step forward. "There was a slight flicker of her gaze toward him during our communication and in a woman like that..."

Sardaan nodded, stunned at both the fact Fenriis had named him as kinsman and the revelation of Black's interest. Sure, he *was* distantly related to the war commander—they shared a cousin—but to have the male confirm their link in front of the emperor, no less. It was a step up for sure. Then to realize the woman he'd been so affected by had apparently noticed him as well... Black had been so controlled during all the communications that such a lapse was telling.

"Excellent!" The emperor beamed. "Sardaan K'Vass, you will be the major general's escort for this evening. I want you to stick to her like *pelaranss.* Ply her with drink and get into her bed. If you can get her to accept your claim over her, even better. Do not fail us on this. Understand?"

"Yes, sire," he said with a bow. This time he

couldn't stop the slow grin that spread over his face. Seduce the woman of his dreams with the emperor's blessing? He was *all* over that.

"I won't let you down. She'll be mine before sunrise."

2

"Well, don't you scrub up well?"

Danielle Black, Dani to the rare few she called friends, grinned at the wolf-whistle as she entered the shuttle bay dressed for dinner aboard the Latharian vessel.

Shannon Taylor, her second in command, leaned one shoulder against the shuttlecraft that would take Dani over to the alien vessel. She was still in her duty uniform, the rank of Lieutenant Colonel glinting at her collar. Like Dani, she was career army, practically born and bred into uniform. Also like Dani, she'd been a colony brat, going into service as soon as she'd hit sixteen to escape a life of menial work in the colony factories. Neither of them had looked back.

"Sexy boss lady," Shannon winked as she pushed off and approached. "You'll have them eating out of your hand. You mark my words."

With a grin, Dani did a little twirl to show off. The girlish movement was one she'd only make while alone with someone she trusted. She looked good in her formal uniform, the military collared jacket fitting her like a glove over a tailored sheath dress that made the best of her trim figure. With her hair neatly slicked back and in high heels, she felt good too.

"Thanks. I certainly hope so," she replied, her amusement dying away in the face of the seriousness of her visit to the alien ship. "I need to bring Cole back or command will have my head on a damn plate."

Of all the damn fool things her previous superior officer, Hopkins, had done while in command, nothing came close to the sheer stupidity of mounting an attack on an alien opponent with superior technology. Not only had he pissed off a species who could wipe out humanity without a second thought, he'd also managed to get himself *and* the vice president captured into the bargain.

Which meant she now had to sort that shit show out, up to and including negotiating the release of the captives... all from a severely reduced position of strength. Great. Just fucking great.

Shannon's brow creased. "I'm really not sure this is a good idea, boss. You're the IC... let me go instead."

Dani shook her head. "No. I made a connection with that commander the last time we spoke. I don't want to risk a loss of confidence, especially as it could jeopardize us getting Cole back."

Shannon lifted an eyebrow, her expression blank. "And it has nothing to do with the fact the place is filled to the brim with hot as hell men?"

Dani flipped her the bird. "The day a guy turns my head is the day I resign my commission. They're pretty and all... but I've yet to meet a guy that can keep up with me."

For some reason, as she said it, an image of one of the alien warriors filled her mind. Not the commander—he was all darkness and intent focus —but one of the others. The first man she'd spoken to when she'd commed their ship after she'd realized Hopkins' plan had become the complete FUBAR she'd told him it would be. Tall, broad-shouldered and handsome as sin, with a shock of dirty blond hair pulled back, his bright blue eyes had haunted her sleep since.

Quickly, she shook her head to clear the image. She didn't do relationships. Ever. As soon as she made the mistake of falling for someone, they left, died, or simply moved to a new posting on the other side of the galaxy. It all amounted to the same thing. Her being alone.

So if she was going to end up that way, she might as well start the same way.

"Huh. You just make sure you stick to that. Okay? I've heard stories about their seduction techniques," Shannon commented as she walked with Dani toward the back of the shuttle where the loading ramp was open.

There was no pilot. A qualified combat pilot herself, Dani didn't need one, nor would she risk someone else's life just in case the Lathar weren't on the level.

This time it was Dani's turn to raise an eyebrow. "And just how do you know that? None of the women the Lathar took the first time have returned, so we're literally flying in the dark on what they, and their seduction techniques, are like."

And they were. So far, even though the return of women who hadn't accepted Latharian "mates" was on the negotiation table, none had yet made their way back to the Terran systems. So, what they actually knew about the Lathar was very little.

But Shannon's expression didn't alter. "Two words... Jane. Allen."

Dani pursed her lips for a second. "Okay. I'll give you that one."

Jane Allen was a marine legend, as hard as nails and not a woman to be easily seduced. The fact that she was one of the women who had married a Latharian warrior had sent ripples of shock throughout the military community. Dani had been sure she'd have gone down fighting rather than cozy it up with an alien lover.

"So... don't you dare go and do a Jane on me, okay? I'd hate to have to write you up as TSTL." Shannon winked, patting the side of the shuttle as she pushed off.

"Huh? What the fuck does TSTL mean?" Dani called after the other woman. Shannon was always making up her own codes.

"Too stupid to live. Because you'd have to be to let some sexy bit of stuff take you down," Shannon called back over her shoulder, bright red hair a flag against the gray bulkheads as she left the shuttle bay.

Dani shook her head with a chuckle as she

triggered the ramp. Shannon was one of her closest friends, but she had the strangest sense of humor. The image of the sexy alien pushed to the front of her mind again and she shook it away.

"Yeah, not happening," she muttered to herself as she started the shuttle's engines and initiated the launch procedures. "My name's not Jane Allen."

The flight to the alien ship was short, sweet and uneventful, which allowed Dani to concentrate on what she was seeing. The *Veral'vias* was huge and she easily recognized the sleek lines of a warship. One big enough to wipe out the entire human fleet with ease. And it wasn't alone. Her sharp gaze picked out another, just behind it, which had arrived at some point this afternoon.

"Computer, enhance main viewscreen image," she ordered, a frown on her brow as she focused. She needed to pick up as much intel as she could. Even the slightest little thing could aid them in their understanding of the Lathar. "Focus on sections g-five through k-seventeen."

Part of the viewscreen in front of her sectioned off and zoomed in on a view of the second ship's hull. There were marks there that she assumed were in Latharian, but she couldn't read them. A ship designation perhaps?

"Computer, look for similar markings on the *Veral'vias* and compare. See if you can find a match," she ordered, swiping the console in front of her to clear the zoomed section. The shuttle rounded the hull of the large alien ship and she spotted the open shuttle bay looming ahead of her.

"Terran shuttle, this is the Veral'vias," a deep voice announced over the comm as all her propulsion systems suddenly went unresponsive. *"We'll bring you in from here."*

"This is Major General Black. Acknowledged," she replied and sat back in her seat as the alien ship piloted her toward the shuttle bay. The voice had been a new one, not the hottie she'd spoken with before, and she wondered where he'd gone. Probably off shift, doing whatever it was Latharians did when they weren't working. A sense of disappointment filled her. A small part of her, a very small part, wanted to see him again... find out more about him. Like his name.

Putting that thought to the side, she watched as the shuttle approached the open door in the side of the alien vessel. As she got nearer, she realized just how big it was. Her eyes widened. Hell, what did they launch out of there that they needed a door so frigging huge?

Within a minute the shuttle entered its cavernous maw. Dani shifted in her chair, the hair lifting on the back of her neck. Perhaps Shannon had been right. Perhaps this had been a bad idea. She was alone in enemy territory without backup and only the combat dagger sheathed on her thigh to defend herself with...

Shaking off the thought, she took a couple of deep breaths and forced herself into a sense of calmness and ease. *Fake it until you make it, baby...* a lesson she'd learned a long time ago.

She kept her eyes open and the sensors on the shuttle running as they were pulled inside and then gently set down on the deck with a soft bump. Her live stream to the *Defiant* had cut off as soon as they'd gotten within the large alien ship's hull, but the recordings would be of use later.

If they ever let her leave, that was.

The dark thought sent a chill down her spine for a second, but then she shrugged it off. Just a dinner, K'Vass had said. Then, if she wanted to leave, both she and the vice president could.

"Welcome to the *Veral'vias*, Major General Black," the voice said again. "Please disembark. Your escort is waiting for you."

She rose from the pilot's seat and made her way

to the back of the shuttle. A smile quirked her lips. She was more used to jumping out the back of one of these at high altitude in full combat gear rather than waiting for the ramp to descend while dressed for a formal function. Her dress uniform was the nearest she was going to get to being a princess for the day, though, so she'd take it.

But the man standing on the other side of the ramp stole that smile right from her lips and she gaped at him in surprise for a second. The sexy Latharian communications officer stood waiting for her, a hesitant smile on his lips. Her gaze raked him, taking in the well-fitted leather combat uniform that stretched over a heavily muscled body and the hair, shades of grey rather than the dirty blond she'd thought, with its multitudes of braids brushing one broad shoulder.

"Welcome to the *Veral'vias,* Major General," he said with a small bow, offering her his hand. "I'm Sardaan K'Vass, assigned to be your escort for this evening."

He straightened with a frown when she didn't take his hand to help her step off the ramp. "Although, if I am not to your liking, I can arrange for another male to take my place?"

His words startled her into action.

"No! No, not at all. You're fine," she said quickly, adding a smile as she walked forward. Her hand was tiny in his larger one as she stepped off the ramp. "It's not like I have to marry you. Is it? You're just being kind enough to escort me for the evening."

"Indeed, my lady," Sardaan replied.

She didn't have to marry him. No. In fact, he didn't *want* to marry her in the human sense of the word. It was too limiting and simple a ceremony to encompass everything he wanted from her. Mating for a Lathar went far deeper than mere words in some human ceremony and, unlike their concept of marriage, couldn't be put aside by this idea of "divorce." The whole idea of a sundered mating was repugnant to him.

He kept his face level with effort as she placed her tiny hand in his, not prepared for the jolt that ran through him at the merest brush of her fingers. For a moment there, he'd had to hold his breath, the way she'd looked at him making him worry that Fenriis had been wrong and she had no interest in him at all.

But within an instant the odd look had been

gone and she'd stepped forward to take his hand. Heat shot through him at her touch as she took his hand to step down from the shuttle ramp, her nearness doing things to his body that should be illegal.

In the flesh she was tiny, compared to him at least, and slender. The bones of her hand in his were so delicate, he kept his touch light, worried about hurting her. She was dressed differently than he'd seen her before, this time wearing a jacket and a long dress with skirts that flared slightly around her ankles. On her feet...

"Those do not look comfortable for battle," he frowned, eyeing the straps that held the heels to her tiny feet. Goddess, was everything about her small? How on Prime would she take him as a mate?

The answer came in another wave of heat. The lady Amanda was smaller than his human warrioress and Fenriis was not a small male. If the war commander and his mate could manage, given their differences in size, he and his little mate would.

"What?"

Her gaze followed his down to her feet and she laughed, a soft sound that delighted his senses.

"These?" she asked, lifting one foot. "Oh, they're not for combat."

He hadn't let go of her hand, her grip tightening for balance as she showed him the heel. They boosted her height by at least three inches and he suddenly realized their purpose. To make her look taller. Odd. Did she have issues with her height?

"Not unless I'm really unlucky and this evening goes tit—err, belly up real fast."

He looked up, head tilted slightly to the side. "Why would this evening go... 'belly up'?"

Her lips pressed together for a second, lines of stress at the corners of her mouth. It was a fraction of a moment before she smiled to cover, but he caught it.

"Technically I'm alone behind enemy lines. That's not a good place to be in a pair of heels."

Her unusual speech patterns both confused and delighted him. The neuro-translator Isan, their healer, had installed in them all before they'd arrived in the human system meant he could understand the words, but not necessarily all the meanings. He recognized a soldier's patter, able to pick up the meanings of things he didn't understand by context. She was worried about her safety this evening.

A soft growl echoed through his chest and his

hand tightened on hers, pulling her closer before he could stop himself.

"No one will offer you harm here tonight," he declared, the world around him narrowing down to just the two of them. Closer now, the light scent she wore wound around him, pulling him in. "I will protect you and keep you safe."

The temptation to declare himself and demand she accept his claim over her was almost overwhelming, but he held himself in check. Something told him she wasn't a female to be ordered about. That if he did, her defenses would go up.

No, far better to wait until he could get her into a position where she couldn't refuse him.

Amusement washed through her dark eyes—an odd mixture of rich, dark earth and green leaves—and she squeezed his hand. "I appreciate the reassurance, Sardaan. Thank you."

His name on her lips almost stole his breath again. Hot on the heels of his determination that he wouldn't press his claim, he decided he *would* hear his name from her lips again. Screamed in pleasure as he took her to ecstasy over and over again.

"You are very welcome, Major General."

"Please... call me Dani."

Pleasure suffused him as he let go of her hand with reluctance only to offer his arm with a small bow.

He knew her name, of course. It was Danielle. That and many other details about her had been in the file he'd been given to study. Like the fact that she was unmated, with no family... no attachments other than to the men and women she served with.

Jealousy rolled through him at the thought of other men in her life. Did she favor one in particular... how many males would he have to kill to secure his claim on her?

"Dani," he inclined his head, pleased that she'd given him permission to use a pet name rather than her full one. That was a sign of favor amongst humans, or so he'd heard. "A beautiful name for a beautiful lady."

That startled a laugh out of her as they walked from the shuttle bay.

"Oh, you're a charmer." She smiled, patting his arm. "Your commander is a clever one. I'll give him that."

"Oh?" he asked, puffing his chest out in pride as warriors in the corridors saw him with her on his arm, hiding their jealousy that he'd been the one chosen for this mission behind impassive masks.

Given half a chance, every one of them would knife him in the back and take his place.

"Nothing." She leaned in closer, dropping her voice to confidential. "Are there always so many warriors aboard?"

He chuckled at her question, amused that she'd picked up that the corridors were fuller than they normally were. "We're carrying a normal complement, but most of them seem to have decided to stretch their legs at the moment."

He looked down at her with another smile. Gods, his cheeks were going to ache by the end of the night, but he couldn't stop himself. "That's because of you."

"Me?" Her brow furrowed. She hadn't moved away and he liked the heat of her smaller body against his arm.

"Yes. We don't get many females. You're only the..." He counted quickly. "Third human female I've seen."

"Oh," her lips parted on the soft sound and she looked again at the warriors as they passed. "Well... I'm sure they're totally underwhelmed. I'm no supermodel. Just an old soldier."

He frowned. Did she think she wasn't attractive?

"I can't speak for them, but I'm sure they think exactly the same as I do..."

At her curious glance, he paused a little. They were nearly at the doors of the stateroom where the evening event was, and he wanted a little more time alone with her. He drew her closer, risking a small, fleeting touch to tuck the single strand of stray hair back from her delicate features.

"I think you're the most beautiful thing I've ever seen," he admitted, his voice low and gruff. "And I'll challenge... kill... anyone to make you mine."

3

*H*oly... *crap*. She was in trouble with this one if she didn't watch herself.

At the soft touch and raw declaration from the handsome alien warrior, Dani instantly upgraded the threat level he posed from minor to apocalyptic. Had he been human, and she'd met him at a function or in a bar, she'd have been all over him like a bad rash and taken him back to her quarters for a night.

But he wasn't. He was Latharian. Which meant she had to watch her step in case she caused a diplomatic incident.

Before she could answer, the door in front of them swept open and Sardaan led her through it. A group of warriors stood on the other side, and for a moment her breath caught in her throat. There were so many of them, and they were all *huge.* Not letting her feelings show on her face, she kept her breathing measured as the warrior at her side led her toward them.

The biggest Latharian warrior she'd ever seen stood in the middle of them all, flanked by two men who looked so much like him they had to be related. One of them was heavily scarred, the remnants of old injuries easily visible through the open jacket he wore. She didn't look away when he met her gaze, nodding in acknowledgment before looking at the other men briefly and then at the big guy.

"Your Imperial Majesty," she greeted him, using Sardaan's arm to execute a small bow. A full one was out of the question with her dress. Even though the fabric was high-tech polytex, it was designed to streamline her figure and be comfortable for the many hours formal functions lasted, rather than for aerobics and yoga. "A pleasure to meet you."

"My emperor," Sardaan said from her side, confirming her guess that this was, indeed, the emperor of the Lathar, Daaynal. "Please allow me to introduce Major General Danielle Black, commanding officer of the *TSS Defiant* and the human forces in the welcome party. Major General

Black, allow me to introduce his most Imperial Majesty, Daaynal, emperor of all Lathar."

"A pleasure to meet you, Major General. I do apologize for not announcing my arrival sooner, but it appears you figured me out as soon as looking at me," he said with a warm smile, offering a large hand. "A clever one," he commented to Sardaan. "A male would do well to land such a female."

She sucked a breath in at his comment. Did he seriously just suggest that Sardaan try and "land" her? Heat filled her at the thought, but she shoved it away ruthlessly. Despite their history of claiming human females, she wasn't here to be seduced, and it would be a brave man that tried. She was here to do a job and by hell, she'd do it.

"It really wasn't difficult to work out." She smiled back as she shook Daaynal's hand. "We have managed to glean some intelligence on your species. Specifically, that you have two nephews who look incredibly like you, one of whom is a healer."

She nodded toward the two big men flanking the emperor. "Lord Tarrick K'Vass and Lord Healer Laarn, I assume?"

Daaynal's face split into a wide grin as he leaned in to murmur. "Still clever, and you didn't allow yourself to be intimidated by the large number of us even though you are alone, unarmed and outnumbered."

She grinned back, instantly liking the big emperor, and leaned in to reply. "Who says I'm unarmed?"

One of the other warriors with Daaynal started, shooting a glance at Sardaan. Perhaps he should have frisked her before bringing her into the presence of the emperor? She'd liked to have seen him try. Even though the idea of the handsome warrior's big hands on her was an appealing one, there was a time and a place for things like that... which was not here and now.

"I have a combat dagger in a thigh sheath," she told him conspiratorially. "Not that it's going to be much use with all of you in here. But... it makes me feel less naked."

It was perhaps a reckless thing to admit she'd brought a blade into the emperor's presence, but what the hell... It wasn't like she could hide it from the sort of advanced technology they had.

The emperor's expression grew more amused. "Wise move. I'm carrying at least three blades this lot don't know about," he whispered with a jerk of his head toward his retinue. "In our culture, always be prepared. For anything."

"Roger that."

She wasn't sure if it was a warning or an endorsement and didn't get chance to ask as Daaynal straightened up again. "Major General Black, if I could introduce you to the rest of my seniors... then we might be able to get something to eat around here."

HIS LITTLE HUMAN major general was utterly entrancing. And he *would* make her his.

Sardaan sat at Dani's side throughout the formal meal, leaning in every now and then to explain what the dishes were. She was an excellent conversationalist with a quick mind, and he found himself amused when she easily fielded comments meant to overset her from the warriors around them. He was forced to hide his grin when, time after time, she turned such comments back—not in a way that made the warrior look foolish but just to ensure the barbs didn't meet their mark.

Clever. Very clever.

"I understand you are from Sentaris Three, Major General?" Madison Cole, one of the three human women at the table asked. The tall human woman was seated opposite, next to Danaar, in command of the *Veral'vias* after Fenriis' earlier departure. Neither he nor the lord healer had remained for the dinner.

"I am indeed." Dani nodded as she took a sip from her glass and set it down.

Instantly, Sardaan nodded to the warrior behind them to refill it with water. His standing orders were to seduce her, but he didn't want her drunk when he did so. If she was incapable of giving consent, his claim would be null and void.

"It was a beautiful place. I was saddened to hear of its loss," Madison said. "I'm assuming, though, you had left many years prior to its destruction?" For the benefit of the rest of the table she added, "Sentaris Three was one of our major manufacturing colony bases. It was destroyed in a reactor explosion about fifteen years ago."

Sardaan blinked at the news, registering the slight stiffness in Dani's frame. For humans fifteen years was a long time, but not long enough if the tightness about the delicate major general's eyes was any indication.

"It was a beautiful place," Dani agreed, her voice controlled. "Especially during the triple moon-rises. I used to head up there with my sister to watch them after second shift. It was the best time to view them," she added in an aside to Sardaan.

"Oh, I'm so sorry. I didn't realize you had family on the base as well. That was indelicate of me," Madison's embarrassment at her question was obvious but Dani shrugged it off.

"I didn't," she replied with a smile. "My parents died when I was a child. I had one sister, but she wasn't on the base when it exploded."

Had. She spoke about her sister in the past tense but didn't say anything else, lifting her glass again. Thankfully, Madison took the hint, changing subjects smoothly and addressing one of the warriors near her.

Sardaan leaned in, arm over the back of Dani's chair. "Are you okay?"

She slid him a glance, and for a moment he saw past all her shields to the woman within. The sight, and the emotions there, rendered him speechless for a moment. Then she smiled, walls back up in place.

"I'm good. Thank you for asking, though," she murmured, patting his thigh, so close to hers. "You really are a sweet man."

He didn't want to be sweet. Not when the slight touch of her hand sent his body into overdrive. He managed to bite back the hiss that wanted to escape, schooling his body to remain perfectly still as he fought down his erection. All he wanted to do was haul her into his lap and claim her lips, devouring her like a starving man. Screw the rest of the people around the table.

"So, what's it like for an army girl to be commanding a destroyer?" Another voice broke in across the table. He looked up to see the human female at Xaandril's side—Kenna—smiling across at Dani. Unlike some of the pointed barbs from certain warriors around the table, there was no malice in her expression. "I thought you guys were all dirt-bound. Got space sick if you spent too long off planet."

He caught the quirk of Dani's lips. She was obviously amused at the barb, patting her lips with her napkin in an elegant gesture before answering.

"Well, we're adaptable like that." She leaned in toward him, but her comment was obviously meant for Kenna. "Poor thing. It's not her fault... she's a marine. It stands for Muscle always required, Intelligence not essential."

He almost spat the mouthful of *alcaia* wine he'd just taken across the table, snorting and swallowing at the same time.

"What?"

"Hey!" Kenna gasped in protest, amusement in her eyes. "I resemble that remark. I should call you out, settle this once and for all."

Several warriors around the table stopped talking, eyeing the two women with interest. Even Sardaan did. The idea of the two females fighting was... intriguing. And it would allow him to see exactly how Dani fought. That she was a warrior was undeniable... and the very idea fascinated him. She was so tiny. How did she manage?

A warrior further down the table snorted with laughter. "An entertaining interlude on Earth no doubt, pitting females against each other. It's not like they could do any serious damage. They're obviously there to look pretty and then the males take over the real fighting."

All three humans turned to look at him, and Sardaan swore the temperature in the room dropped several degrees.

"Actually, Major General Black has been All-Forces Champion, our most difficult and dangerous military competition, for several years running," Madison, the Terran vice president spoke up, her voice as cold as a cutting arc. "All our military women are just as highly trained and capable as our men. A fact more than a few Lathar have found out to their cost, I believe?"

She threw the comment out to the room as a whole, one eyebrow raised. Sardaan was forced to bite back his grin. The human woman had them there and no mistake. Stories of how the Sentinel women had bested the T'Laat and how one of them had executed that bastard Ishaan F'Naar had sent ripples through the empire.

"A mere fluke," the warrior scoffed, amusement in his voice as he leaned back in his chair. He wasn't K'Vass but from one of the clan ships that had arrived with the emperor. And, as far as Sardaan was concerned, needed a lesson in damn manners. He leaned forward to argue, but Dani put a small hand on his arm.

"You are, of course, entitled to your own opinion," she said calmly. But the words *you're a draanthic idiot* hung in the air unsaid. Sardaan sat back, not bothering to conceal his grin. Point to his beautiful little major general.

"Prove it. I challenge you."

Shit. Sardaan shot upright in his seat at the words, the mood in the room changing in a heartbeat. He hadn't expected any warrior to be impolite enough to challenge anyone tonight of all nights, but the tiniest smug look on the emperor's face made him groan internally.

Of course. This was his cue to step in and protect the lady's honor. To prove himself to her as a potential mate. He eyed the other warrior. Great. He was huge. Couldn't they have found a smaller male?

"I accept the challenge on behalf—," he growled, half out of his seat before a hand on his arm again stopped him in his tracks.

"You will do no such thing, Sardaan K'Vass." Her voice was low but firm, that of a woman who was used to being obeyed. She looked at the warrior in question, her expression hard. "I accept your challenge. When and where?"

From the look of surprise in Daaynal's eyes as he met Sardaan's look, he hadn't expected the human major general's response either.

"Dani..." he turned to her with a soft murmur. "Are you sure this is wise?"

"Absolutely," she said, putting her napkin on the table and standing. She didn't look at him, instead catching Kenna's eyes.

"If I could trouble you for a change of clothing. Mess dress is not the most comfortable thing to fight in..."

The marine grinned as she too stood. "Of course. Just this way."

"Your Majesty!" Sardaan protested, trying to get the emperor on his side. "The major general is our guest. This is impolite and unfair..."

Plus, if anyone was getting her into a circle, it was him, for a claiming bout. Usually they were between males competing for a female's affection, but with the lady in question being a warrior herself...

Daaynal just shrugged and Sardaan knew he wouldn't intervene. What did it matter to him which male claimed Dani? As long as one of them did, it was all the same to the ruthless leader of the Lathar.

He stood, stunned for a moment as he realized there was a very real possibility he might lose the female he wanted before he'd even had a chance to claim her.

Not fucking happening. Not as long as he had breath in his body.

4

"Cool. Yeah, these'll do."

Dani smiled at Kenna as she handed over a pair of leather combats and a tank top. The leather was well worn and so soft she could tell it would move easily with her. The tank had built-in bra support, so she wouldn't have to worry about anything moving that didn't need to be.

"Here, try these."

Dropping the clothing onto a low couch in the side chamber Kenna had pulled her into, she took the boots the marine woman held out and kicked a heel off to measure it against the bottom of her foot. She recognized the type. Standard issue, multi-fit size 2-Z-7. Her size. Even second-hand, they would fit like a glove.

"Yours?" she asked, casting a glance down at Kenna's feet. She wore what had to be Latharian combat boots over her leathers, the buckles and laces halfway up her legs.

"Yeah. Right outta Sentinel Five, baby. All yours, just so I can see you kick Konaat's ass."

Dani snorted as she shrugged out of her formal jacket. "That the big guy's name? Seems a bit of a dick."

Kenna nodded, motioning for Dani to turn around so she could unzip her dress.

"You could say that. Konaat T'Kiis. Stuck in the mud traditionalist. Not as bad as the purists, but just as argumentative."

"You can't fight."

The deep male voice from the doorway made them both look that way. Sardaan, her escort, stood there, his handsome face drawn tight.

"I can, actually. And quite well," she told him as she shrugged out of the dress to her underwear. Instantly he averted his eyes, a flush on his cheeks.

She chuckled. "Don't tell me the Lathar are prudish?"

"No," he bit out a growl, venturing a look down and meeting her eyes as she pulled the leathers on. "Just didn't expect you to bare yourself right in front of me. Do you do that with all males you just met?"

She just smiled and continued dressing. "Military women are not shy, handsome. Can't be when you live in barracks."

"You sleep in the same room as males of your species?" He blinked, shock on his handsome features. "How do you stop them claiming you any time they want?"

Dani looked over at Kenna for clarification.

"Claiming... When a Latharian male wants a woman, he 'claims' her. It's like engagement and marriage all rolled into one. They don't really do casual sex," the marine explained.

"Yeah, what she said." He stalked toward her, stopping just shy of her being able to feel his body heat against hers. She pulled the tank top on and reached for the boots.

"How do you stop males who want you?"

She shrugged as she put the boots on. As expected, they reformed around her feet perfectly. "Because if they were ever stupid enough to try it, I'd relocate their male equipment to where the sun doesn't shine. And make them thank me for it."

"Huh?" His expression revealed his confusion, so Kenna stepped in.

"She'd rip their dick and balls off and shove them up their asses."

"OH!"

Dani smothered her chuckle as she turned to Kenna, pulling on combat gloves the other woman had also provided. Bunching her fists, she bumped them against the marine woman's.

"Live hard, die young..." she murmured, grinning as Kenna's voice joined hers in the chorus. *"Take as many of the bastards with you as you can."*

"You're both fucking crazy," the big Latharian muttered, looking at them in something akin to horror.

"Death or glory," Dani winked as she walked past him.

As soon as she stepped into the main hall, all amusement dropped from her face. The dining table had been removed and warriors crowded the edges of the walls. There was even a circle marked on the floor. Impressive how they'd arranged it all so quickly. She could almost believe it was a setup to get her to fight.

Her opponent, Konaat T'Kiis, was already in the circle, grinning as he spotted her in the doorway.

"Come in here, female, and let me show you how it's done."

"The T'Kiis are traditional fighters," Sardaan said in a low voice as he walked at her side. "He'll try to pull you in and use his strength to overpower you. Stay out of range and for goddess' sake, don't let him take you down to the floor. You won't win there. He's too big."

He stopped her with a hard hand on her arm. "Please... Let me take your place. You can't win this. And I don't want you to lose."

She favored him with a hard look, allowing the edge of her anger to show. "Full of confidence in my abilities. Aren't you? Listen, I've been on more battlefields than you've had hot dinners, sunshine, and now I have something to prove to him, and," she jabbed him in the center of his chest, "to you. Because you don't think I can do it."

Whirling on her heel, she entered the circle and stopped opposite Konaat. He looked her up and down.

"I'm missing dessert for this, asshole," she snarled at him. "So let's get this done and I can try this chocolate cake of yours everyone goes on about."

Konaat cracked his knuckles, slamming one beefy fist into the other hand. "I might treat you, after I'm finished with you in my bed." There was a gasp at his announcement and Sardaan surged forward, only to be held back by two big men.

"*No!* This is not a claiming bout!" he shouted, trying to get the emperor's attention. "That should have been announced before she stepped into the circle!"

"I agree. This really is not appropriate," Madison spoke up. "Major General?"

Dani danced lightly on the spot as she loosened up all her muscles, aware they were all watching her.

"I got this, ma'am."

"Very well," Daaynal's deep voice announced. "The bout continues. Major General... Commander... in your own time."

Dani let everything else fall away as she concentrated on her opponent. Konaat was tall and heavily muscled, a behemoth of a man. Like Sardaan said, she'd have to be careful not to let him get ahold of her or let him get too close or she was toast. The last thing she wanted was to end up some alien asshole's bride.

"*Draanth's sake,*" Sardaan muttered, prowling the edge of the circle as the tiny woman inside paced around the bigger Latharian. Fear hit him hard and fast. She was going to get hurt. Badly. And worse, when Konaat beat her, he'd get to claim her as his mate.

She's mine, his instincts snarled. And she was. She'd been his from the moment he'd seen her on that viewscreen. He felt the pull toward her. She had to be his. The goddess wouldn't have been so cruel as to show her to him only to snatch her away again. And Konaat wasn't a gentle male. The thought of his delicate Dani in the big male's bed... it made him sick to his stomach.

"Don't panic. She's got this," Kenna said quietly.

He paused and looked at her in surprise. He hadn't heard her sneak up on him and not many could. Not on him anyway. Riis maybe, the male was as clueless as a *dronat* in a forest.

"How?" he demanded, turning to the human woman, his voice low and urgent. "Tell me just *how* she's got this! He's twice her weight, nearly twice as tall. He'll kill her! Or worse."

Kenna folded her arms, that maddening little smile on her lips. "She's won the All-Trial *seven* times, handsome. She can handle one little fight. Easy."

"That's a human thing," he threw back, raking a

hand through his hair. "I heard that before, but what does it *mean?*"

"The All-Trial?" Kenna raised one eyebrow. "It's a series of seven trials, of agility, strategy and endurance. Competitors are drawn from all our service branches to battle it out over a week on the wastes of Jentaris Four. It's tough, like real tough. Not only do those competing have to master the challenges, but they have to do it while others try and take them out of the competition."

Sardaan blinked. "They have to fight others at the same time?"

Kenna nodded. "It's totally no holds barred, absolutely brutal. People have died competing. I only did it the one year, ranked at thirty-four. Never again."

He turned to assess the slender female in the center of the ring with new eyes.

"Seven times reigning champion," Kenna leaned in to whisper. "Your guy is fucking toast."

He folded his arms, a less than impressed look on his face. He hoped she was right, like *really* hoped she was right.

"Come on then, little female," Konaat taunted, his arms spread widely as he mocked the woman in front of him. "Or are you too scared? We can call this off and I'll claim you in my bed instead."

Sardaan's lip had begun to curl back into a snarl, but before he could complete the sound, Dani moved in for the attack. His jaw dropped open at her speed as she darted in. Before Konaat had the chance to block or defend himself, she'd landed three strikes, rapid fire blows to his ribcage before a stinging hook that bloodied his nose.

"Oh my lady..." he breathed in awe as she broke away, dancing lightly on her feet and out of Konaat's range.

"Told you," Kenna chuckled. "*Toast.*"

"Oh, you little... *draanthic,*" Konaat hissed, wiping the blood off his face with irritation. His anger at being shown up so publicly was palpable. "I'll make you pay for that."

"Anytime, sweetheart," Dani threw back as she rolled her shoulder, dancing lightly on her feet on the opposite side of the circle.

No, Sardaan realized, not danced. She *prowled.* Like a predator. A slender, delicate predator, but a predator all the same. He watched, forced to admire her technique as she methodically tested Konaat's defenses and range with lighting fast strikes. She kept out of range all the time, making the big warrior growl every time he lunged. He tried to tangle her up in his hold and missed.

It didn't help that she slapped him as he passed, every time, the stinging, contemptuous blows designed to enrage. *Clever*, Sardaan thought. Make the bigger warrior lose his temper and focus.

It worked. Well.

Konaat roared in fury and charged. Half the warriors around the circle winced at the sloppiness of the move, his guard lazy on the left-hand side. The small human dropped the act and moved in for the kill.

Her movements were precise—surgical as she moved like a lethal, well-oiled machine. Ducking under Konaat's wild punch, she hammered two hard punches into his ribs, the controlled movement one that spoke of long experience. The sharp crack that rolled around the room said she'd broken a rib.

Konaat gasped, staggering to the side a bit before getting himself back together. It didn't take long. Sloppy warriors didn't last long in the empire, especially not at Konaat's standing. He snarled and turned on her again.

She didn't quail in the face of his attack, merely dropping to the ground. A hard sweep of her leg took out one of the big warrior's and he stumbled again. She leaped to her feet and moved in, a flurry of blows aimed at his head and neck. He bellowed, bringing his arms up to guard, but he couldn't block them all.

Sardaan sucked his breath in as one blow snuck through, catching the big male square in the face. His head snapped back on his neck and he swayed, a stunned look on his face.

"Yes!" Sardaan hissed, surging forward to the very edge of the circle. She was winning. Gods, he would never have believed it possible, but she was actually winning against Konaat.

Make that won.

Another flurry of blows and the big male was done. Blood streaming from his nose, he toppled over backward like a felled tree. Dani stepped back, her stance still wary in case Konaat managed to make it to his feet again. He didn't, collapsing onto the floor with a groan.

The crowd around the circle roared. Even though their warrior had lost, they didn't care. Latharian culture revered strength and ability and the human woman, tiny as she was, had proved to be the better warrior. That was all they cared about.

"An excellent fight! Well done, Major General!" Daaynal beamed in approval, clapping, but something about the set of his body put Sardaan on high alert. He watched the big emperor like a hawk.

There. The slight flicker of his gaze toward a warrior on the other side of the circle and he realized what was going on. They were going to keep throwing warriors in the circle until she was worn down and tired... until she lost to someone.

He growled. That someone was going to be him.

Stepping into the ring, he announced in a loud voice. "I challenge Major General Black for the right of claiming."

5

*D*ani froze as the big alien warrior stepped into the ring with her. A shiver raced down her spine at the hard look on his face. He wasn't playing around or being civil anymore. This was serious. *He* was serious. She swallowed, her suddenly dry throat clicking.

She needed to win this. Or he would own her. Claim her. Not happening.

"Oh, this is bullshit!"

"Your Majesty, I really must protest!" Kenna and Madison cried at the same time.

Dani rolled her shoulders, an eye on her new opponent even as Madison pushed forward to put a hand on Daaynal's.

"Your Majesty," her voice was tight, urgent.

"Surely Major General Black has proven that our women fight just as well as your men. Putting her in with a fresh opponent seems a little... unfair, wouldn't you say?"

Everyone in the room froze as Daaynal looked down at Madison's hand.

Dani sucked in a quick breath. Shit, did they have rules against touching the boss or something? She hoped not. She needed to get Madison out of here in one piece or her head was going to be on the chopping block with command. *How* she was going to do that when she was unarmed against a whole ship full of alien warriors she had no clue. Orders from command rarely made sense.

Madison snatched her hand back, skin pale, and the emperor shook his head.

"Both combatants are already within the circle. The challenge will proceed."

Dani caught her opponent's gaze with a hard look of her own. If he thought she'd go easy on him because he'd been her escort, or because she thought he was good-looking, he had another think coming. She wasn't so easily swayed, despite what the Lathar might think about human women. Or humanity in general.

She'd seen in a heartbeat what Madison hadn't,

that this was a setup, but not quickly enough to get them both out of harm's way. Now she could only save one of them.

"I'm good with going ahead, on one condition." Her words were directed to Daaynal. He lifted a hand to halt the fight for a moment.

"What condition?"

Dani's heart rate was above normal waiting for his answer. She needed him to agree to this or the whole plan fell apart.

"That whatever the outcome of this match," she motioned between herself and the Latharian warrior in front of her. "The vice president is free to return to the *Defiant.*"

The quick look of surprise that flared in the backs of the emperor's eyes made her bite back a smile of triumph. The possibility that she might sacrifice herself to gain something of greater importance obviously hadn't occurred to him. Good. Humanity had few enough advantages against the Lathar. At least, if they could keep the alien race guessing, that was something.

A hush fell over the room as she waited for Daaynal to reply. She held her breath. Then he nodded.

"Agreed. Should the vice president *wish* to leave,

of course." His voice rose over the sound of a nearby warrior's protest. Dani ignored the ruckus, her gaze locked to the emperor's, and then she nodded.

"Thank you."

He inclined his head and, with a motion of his hand, indicated that the fight should continue.

She turned back to her opponent, making sure to keep her weight lightly on the balls of her feet as she considered him. Unlike Konaat, he didn't dance around or try and impress her with fancy moves. Instead, he adopted a guard position, his attention focused on her.

Confident, but not overly so. That made him far more dangerous. Plus, he'd already seen her fight once, so the same moves wouldn't work on him. Thankfully she hadn't had to use even a fraction of her available repertoire on Konaat.

Keeping her weight balanced and ready for anything, she circled him. He was tall and well-muscled, with the kind of build that made women sit up and take notice. His movements were easy and graceful, indicating he'd had a shit load of training.

Nothing said more, however, than the multitude of braids hanging over one shoulder. They practically filled the side of his head and she knew each indicated a battle honor. They were the

Latharian version of medals. Few men in the crowd around them had so many.

Great job, Dani, she told herself. *You just had to go and pick some kind of bloody alien hero.*

Putting the thought from her mind, she concentrated, and the room around them fell away as she and the alien warrior sized each other up.

When he attacked, it was fast and low. She barely had time to catch her breath as he rushed in. His fist flashed in the air by her head and she lifted her arm to block. Protecting her head, she absorbed the blow across her hunched shoulder. Then she twisted and lashed out with a powerful twist of her torso.

Her fist caught him in the side of his ribcage, sneaking through the guard he tried to get into place to land with a satisfying "thud." He grunted, breaking away to salute her with two fingers to his temple. She winked at him, amused that the gesture crossed species and planets.

But his hard expression said she wouldn't be able to pull the same trick on him twice. And she couldn't. Her attack was met with fierce resistance, and she swore mentally as each kick and punch was met with a block or a counterattack. Such a big man should not be able to move so quickly. No way. No how.

He was though. And she was forced to really move it up, using every ounce of skill to stop him. But, like in any fight, she had to let some blows through. One to her hip to avoid a more dangerous one to her head. A kick to her thigh in favor of blocking a punch to her kidneys. He was the same, trading taking a less damaging blow to block something that would have stopped the fight dead and given her the victory.

Those blows mounted up, though, and it wasn't long before they were both breathing heavily, breaking away after each contact and exchange to circle each other slowly.

"Might as well give it up, Major General." His voice was low and steady as he watched her. "You can't win this. I'll just wear you down."

She shrugged, her fists tight and her stance solid as she mirrored his movements. "We'll see."

His next attack was fast and ruthless. She pressed her lips together as she twisted and turned, trying to be some kind of superhero to stay out of the way of his fists. But the fast pace had taken its toll. She was a hair too slow on a block and a lucky blow crept through, a fist like a hammer slamming into her side.

She clenched her teeth as agony exploded

through her side, stealing her breath for an instant. Nausea rose, her muscles locking up as she fought the sensation down. She had to keep fighting. There was no other option. But in the split second it took her to get the pain under control, he had her.

His big body wrapped around hers, and he took her to the ground, wrapping her up. He didn't pin her down as she would have thought, but instead with his legs clamped around her hips and his big arm around her neck, he forced her spine into a hard curve.

Anger crashed through her and she struggled against him. He hissed but easily held on, his words soft in her ear.

"Shh, Dani, it's okay. Calm down. I'm not going to hurt you."

His deep voice whispered against the side of her throat, lifting the fine hairs there, and she froze in his hold. Not giving up but listening to him.

"Please, listen to me," he murmured. "They're not going to let you out of this circle, not without you being claimed by one of us. That's been the plan all along. Don't you realize? Stop fighting and I promise I'll look after you."

She growled and jerked against him, still fighting.

He sighed. "I didn't want to hurt you. Remember that, okay?" He tightened his arm. Her breath came in short gasps as he cut off her air supply. She tried to hold out against him, but despite her intentions to the contrary, she felt herself starting to sag against him, and her world went gray. Relaxing into Sardaan's hold, she let the darkness wash over her.

She'd lost. But it didn't matter.

The vice president was going home.

TRIUMPH RAGED through him as she relaxed. He'd won. The victory was his.

He eased up on his arm lock around her neck, only for the lack of resistance in her body to send ice down his spine. She hadn't relaxed. She was unconscious.

"*Draanth's* sake, Dani," Sardaan hissed. Rather than yield to him, she'd allowed him to choke her out. "Fucking stubborn female."

Turning her over, he checked her vitals quickly. She was still breathing and her heart beat strongly against his fingers when he pushed them against the side of her throat. Relief filled him that he hadn't hurt her, or worse, followed by frustration. She'd put herself in harm's way rather than give in. Were all Earth females so stubborn?

"Dani... wake up. Dani?" he murmured, concern filling him when she didn't stir.

Scooping her up into his arms, he stood with fluid grace, looking at the warriors crowded around him. Even the emperor looked concerned at the sight of the tiny female limp in Sardaan's arms.

"Is she okay?"

Kenna was by his side in an instant, two fingers against Dani's throat to check for a pulse the same as he had. Grunting in satisfaction, she moved on, using a gentle thumb to roll back one of the smaller woman's eyelids. "No burst vessels. I think you just knocked her out."

"I'll be the judge of that," a deep voice argued, warriors moving out of the way as Isan shouldered his way through.

"Bloody human females think they know everything," he groused as he reached them, sliding a glare at Kenna. She glared right on back until he turned his head. Scars ran down the side of his face and neck, disappearing under the leather combat jacket he wore.

She nodded to the healer and backed off. "Sorry, old habits. Combat medic," she murmured.

Isan grunted in the back of his throat as he reached Sardaan's side. "Bring her through here." He motioned, glaring at the warriors around them. "Get your asses out of the way. Injured coming through!"

"Lay her down," he ordered as Sardaan carried her through into the same antechamber she'd changed in for the challenge fights. Her human uniform was still draped over the chair by the couch.

Sardaan laid her down as gently as he could, his worried gaze sweeping over her as he stepped back to let the healer take over.

Gods, she was so tiny. He hadn't realized quite how small she was. Awake, her personality made her seem bigger than she was. Somehow. He still hadn't figured out how she did that. But unconscious... she was so delicate. Worry and guilt hit him hard and fast. Shit, he could have *really* hurt her. He was bigger. Stronger. There was no way he should have gotten into that circle with her.

"Will she be okay?" he asked Isan.

The healer didn't reply at first, his attention on the scanning wand he ran slowly over her body. Sardaan had used them often himself. Usually on the younglings who needed extra training when they got injured. Which was a lot. While not as comprehensive as the full diagnostic beds in the medbay, it would pick up any issues that needed further investigation.

"Isan?" he growled in frustration. Gods, help him, he'd shake the *draanthic* healer if he didn't need him to treat Dani.

"Yes, yes... she's fine," the healer replied, still scanning. "Bear with me, though. She's only the second one I've seen. I want to make sure I don't miss anything."

Sardaan nodded, even though the healer wasn't looking at him, and folded his arms. He hid his relief that she was okay. That he hadn't inadvertently hurt her. More scans were better. Much better.

"Seeing some old injuries, healed." Isan kept up a running commentary. "She's fully developed, an adult of her species. I wasn't sure because of her size."

"Her file said she was in her forties," Sardaan broke in. "Plenty old enough to have reached adulthood."

Isan waved dismissively. "They're an offshoot. We don't know how they develop. Latharian cellular regeneration was increased generations ago, which slowed our aging process."

"I don't think humans have that sort of advanced

technology..." Sardaan started but then frowned. "Does that mean that their lifespans are shorter?"

Isan nodded. "Much. But it's a quick genetic fix."

Sardaan shoved a hand through his hair. His breath hissed out from between his lips as relief rolled through him. The idea that her lifespan might be much shorter than his hadn't occurred to him until that moment, and the thought of losing her so soon scared him right down to his boots.

He had bigger problems though. He had what he wanted. He'd won the bout and the delicate human major general was his by right of claiming. But she hadn't agreed to it. She'd been tricked into the circle for the fight. Her hand had been forced, even though he'd had no option. He couldn't risk her being claimed by another.

But... she didn't *want* to be with him.

So what did he do now?

He scrubbed at the light stubble on his jaw. He couldn't let her go, that was for sure. Even if he hadn't had orders from the emperor to seduce her anyway, he... couldn't let her go. Just couldn't. She was *his*. Every instinct he had rejected the idea of letting her go. Ever.

But if she wouldn't accept him? His mood, already grim because of her current condition, hit rock bottom. For a second, his gaze landed on Isan's broad back. He could always ask the healer to give her something that would make her more... pliable. More accepting of him. *Ker'ann.*

His lip curled back in disgust. At himself. Just thinking about drugging her so she would accept him was shameful. He was a warrior. An honorable male. He didn't want to drug his mate into his bed. He wanted her to *want* to be there. To be as eager for his touch and his body as he was for hers.

No. He wouldn't drug her and he couldn't send her back to her ship. So what the *draanth* was he to do?

He could make her fall in love with him...

The thought hit him like a bolt out of the blue and he stood there, like a *deearin* that had been caught in the lights of a skitter. Goddess, he could... His mission was seduction after all. But instead of just her body, all he had to do was seduce her mind as well and make her fall in love with him.

He smiled slowly to himself, satisfied with his plan, as Isan folded the scanner wand away and stood up.

"Well, she's fit and healthy," the healer reported. "Small, but it doesn't appear to be due to any deformity. They just *are* that small. She has evidence of old injuries... bone breaks and scars. She's been a warrior for a long time from the looks of it. But fit and healthy. And... fertile."

Sardaan blinked, surprised. "I hadn't even thought about offspring."

Isan's lips curved into a small smile and he clapped Sardaan on the shoulder. "And that is why I'm the healer and you're on track to war commander. Isn't it? You don't need so many brains for that. Now take your mate and get out of here. She'll probably want some rest and relaxation after all this exertion."

6

"I'm good. I don't need any rest," Dani argued in a mumble.

She'd clawed her way back to consciousness to the sound of deep male voices. A rush of warmth filled her at one of them, but in the cotton wool between asleep and awake, she wasn't sure why. Just that she liked it and felt safe when hearing it.

The memory of being beaten in the fight hit next. She was on the Latharian vessel... and she'd lost. Shame hit, her cheeks burning as she lay there, no strength in her body as she tried to work out what the hell to do next. *How had this happened?*

She'd lost to Sardaan. But he hadn't hurt her. A quick mental check of her body revealed no new areas of pain. Some bruising and muscle aches but nothing that immediately flagged as an issue. She could fight if she had to.

Her mind went back over the fight. She replayed it all, move by move, like clips from a movie flashing in her mind. She was good, quick and agile. But he was bigger. Stronger. He'd beaten her with brute strength. She should never have let the fight hit the floor. That had been her big mistake.

They're not going to let you out of this circle, not without you being claimed by one of us. That's been the plan all along.

His words came back to her and she sagged against the soft surface she lay on, numbness filling her. She fought it back, thinking quickly. This was just a setback. That was all. The mission—to learn more about the Lathar—was still active. She just had to adjust the basis she approached it from. In fact, if she thought about it, she was in a far better situation to observe them now than before. Now, she was actually part of their culture and society. That was an unprecedented level of access.

With a groan, she opened her eyes and rolled to her side, legs over the side of the couch as she sat up. There were just two alien men in the room with her.

Sardaan and another one, with similar gray-ash hair. It wasn't a true blond, she realized, but more a gray. Not the gray of age—it was too vibrant and shiny. Healthy. They were both men in the prime of their lives.

The other man was scarred, one of their healers, and she inclined her head to him. "Thank you, Doctor."

He tilted his head to the side, a small smile creasing his lips before he nodded in acknowledgment. That was something she'd noticed about them. They had delightful, almost old country manners.

"You are most welcome. You have some cuts and bruises, but no other damage. *However,*" he said, raising his voice over Sardaan's pointed rumbling and looks toward the door, "if you start with a headache, feel sick, have any balan—"

She chuckled. "I'm more than familiar with the signs of a concussion, Doc. Don't worry, I'll call you if I feel bad. Promise."

"She says she feels fine. You say she's fine. Leave us," Sardaan growled, his abrupt manner with the healer making Dani cut a quick glance at him as he bundled the other man out of the room.

"There was no need to be rude to him," she said as he walked back toward her.

Walked was the wrong word. Stalked... That was the only word that fit the tension in Sardaan's big frame as he approached her, his blue gaze intent on hers.

She was his wife. Or, the Latharian version of it at least, and he hadn't even bought her dinner or gotten her drunk. *Crap.*

"So... you claimed me. What exactly does that mean?"

She knew what it meant, but she needed something to kick off this conversation. Something to start with so she could find a workable solution. One thing was for sure. She was *so* not leaping into bed with him.

His tight smile warned her he wasn't fooled by her act. "Exactly what you think it means."

She held her ground, matching him look for look as he stopped just in front of her. So close she could take a deep breath and they'd be touching. A shiver rolled through her. He was so damn *big*. How had she missed that?

"I don't know what it means. We don't have much on your species..."

A lie, but not entirely inaccurate. They didn't

have *much* on the Lathar, just a few bits and pieces they'd managed to glean from communications they'd intercepted and those the Sentinel women had sent back.

He grunted, his jaw set as he looked down at her.

"You're mine," he said bluntly. "My mate. My wife, as humans would say."

Yeah, that's what she thought it meant. Crap. She searched his face. His tight expression said he was serious.

"I don't suppose you'd accept a marriage of convenience. Would you?" she tried with a small smile.

The small growl that came from the back of his throat said no, in the sexiest way she'd ever heard.

"I have no clue what that is," he admitted, "but if it means you leaving or being apart from me in any way, shape or form, then no."

Balls. That was that plan out of the water.

"Not necessarily leaving," she tried it anyway, "but married in name only. I could stay here for however long we're together, and it just be on paper."

"On paper? You mean we pretend? *Draanth* no," he spat, anger in his voice.

Her breath escaped her lungs in a quick gasp as

he grabbed her upper arms. "I claimed you. You're mine. In *every* sense of the word."

She schooled herself not to fight back. It wouldn't do her any good to fight back. He'd already proven that. She had agreed to this when she'd stayed in that ring, whatever it meant...

No, she knew what it meant. It meant sleeping with him. Sharing his bed.

"Okay. Not on paper," she agreed, her voice calm and soothing. "But I need time. Human women need to have feelings for their lovers—"

His lips quirked as he cut her off. "Try again. I've read your histories. Seen this... *porn*."

She barked a laugh. Why didn't it surprise her that the Lathar knew about porn?

"That is *not* real life. Some stuff, the better written stuff is sexy, but there's other kinds that are..." she shuddered. "It's sick, designed for sick minds. Okay, how about *I* need time? Please?"

The last word was soft and not far off a plea, her expression as entreating as she could make it. "I haven't had a relationship for a long time, and now we're married? It's going to take some getting used to."

He slid a hand around her waist to pull her closer.

Her hands spread over his broad chest, half revealed by the open jacket of his uniform, as she tried to keep some distance between them. But he didn't allow that and pulled her flush against his large, hard body.

"Alright, but I want something in return."

She held herself still in his embrace, trying not to be seduced by the feel of him against her or the thick, semi-hard bar of his cock pressed against her softer stomach. Fucking hell, if that was a semi... he was *huge*.

"What?"

He dipped his head, words whispered against her lips.

"I want a kiss."

Then his lips covered hers. Warm and firm. He fused his mouth to hers, the meeting of their lips a sensual experience she hadn't anticipated. Expecting to have to hold herself still under the onslaught of a man who hadn't seen a woman of his own species in forever, she instead found herself kissed, and well. By someone who apparently... no, make that definitely, knew how.

He moved, pulling back so his lips grazed hers—exploring and enticing her to open up to him. The soft brush of his mouth against hers made her shiver, a temptation she tried like hell to hold out against.

He didn't hold back, tilting his head to the side to deepen the kiss. His arm tightened around her waist, open hand sliding over the back of her hips as his free hand cupped her cheek gently. The soft brush of his thumb against her jaw made her shiver and weaken, her lips parting in subconscious invitation.

With a growl, he took her up on the offer, seducing her with soft nibbles and nips of her lower lip until she clutched at his upper arms. She fought her own reactions as much as she fought him. Then he covered her mouth, devouring her lips as he plundered the softness within with hard sweeps and slides of his tongue against hers.

She moaned softly, unable to hold out against him. Pleasure rolled through her body as she pressed into his embrace, her hands sliding up to around his neck and the fingers of one hand spearing into his hair to hold him to her.

He broke the kiss, smiling against her lips.

"No, I don't think any marriage between us will *just* be in name. But yes, I will give you time. Be warned, though, my patience is finite."

. . .

OH MY GOD. After all her pretty words and reassurances to herself, she'd forgotten them all as soon as he touched her. Dani kicked herself as Sardaan led her out of the antechamber by another door, not re-entering the main hall.

"Wait," she argued, looking back across the room. "What about the vice president? She was supposed to be returned to the *Defiant*. How do I know that has happened?"

The large alien paused, framed in the doorway. Everything here was built on a bigger scale to accommodate the Lathars' larger size, but even so, he almost filled it. He turned to look over his shoulder at her, one eyebrow raised.

"It will be done. We are an honorable people."

She snorted. "Yeah, right. You want me to believe you after that setup in the circle?"

He had the grace to look discomforted, rubbing at the back of his neck.

"I had no part in that—" He seemed like he was about to say something else but then cut himself off. "You have my word. I will make sure she is returned to the *Defiant* as was agreed."

She didn't have any option but to agree with him, her nod short and jerky. "Thank you."

"You're welcome. This way, please."

Grabbing her formal uniform and heels, she hurried after him. The corridors he walked her down all looked the same. Smooth walls and floors. She counted her steps and made a note of which turns they took in case she needed to find her way back.

Before too long, though, she realized there was simply too much distance between the hall and wherever he was taking her for her to get back without being detected. And... there were the robots.

Standing motionless in alcoves along the corridor walls, they gave her the heebie-jeebies. She'd seen them in action on the footage sent from the Sentinel before they'd lost communication, and they were like silver-skinned devils. Tall and bulky, they looked like they'd be slow and clunky, but the reality was far different. The footage she'd seen proved they were blindingly fast and graceful, armed with both lethal claws and laser weaponry.

"Your shock troops?" she asked, motioning to one as they passed. They looked inactive, but at her movement, the robot's eye lit up, tracking her. She jumped, biting back her gasp of surprise. "Shit, are they online?"

Eyes still on the robot in case it launched itself from its alcove, she drew closer to him. The movement was nothing to do with being scared, she rationalized. He was Latharian, so presumably not considered a threat. And even if not, if the robot went loco, he was the bigger target. She could run while it shredded him.

"Not all of them, no," he looked down at her by his side. "Usually there's one pilot for each section, keeping the avatars on standby ready mode in case they're needed for use. They take a lot to boot up from cold, so the pilot skips between each, checking the power levels and connections while watching out for any issues that might need maintenance."

"Uh-huh," she nodded, trying to look calm and professional, but something about the big machines hooked right into the fear centers of her brain, her body flooding with adrenaline. Fight or flight syndrome, she recognized it easily, battled her to remain calm.

"It won't harm you," Sardaan said, his voice deep and reassuring. "The pilot will know by now you're my mate. But... I wouldn't go wandering off on your own. One of these will bring you back to me."

She shot him a glance, eyes narrowing. No information they had on the Lathar mentioned that they were telepathic. So how could he know she'd been noting everything with the possibility of escape...

He chuckled. "Fairly obvious you were memorizing the route, beautiful. Intelligence gathering won't do you any good."

She clamped her lips shut, not prepared to argue with him on that point. Humanity were not Lathar. Even if Earth had originally been seeded by a lost expedition as they claimed, the Lathar were like an absent biological parent. They'd managed without them for all of human history. They had their own identity now, and they didn't need bio-dad storming back in to try and take over.

"You know what they say." She shrugged, a nonchalant one-shouldered movement. "You can take the girl out the army, but you can never take the army out of the girl."

He paused so suddenly she almost ran into him. Biting back a gasp, she managed to keep a little space between them. She'd never get used to how damn fast they moved.

Reaching out, he tucked back a strand of hair that had fallen across her face. "I will never understand why your species allows precious females to put themselves in harm's way," he murmured. "Had you been Latharian, you'd never have been allowed to fight. You'd have been looked after and pampered all your life, never wanting for anything."

She snorted again, yanking her head back away from his touch. "Yeah, and I'd have been bored fucking stupid. And there's no 'allowing' humans, especially women... that's the point you guys seem to miss. We do what the fuck we want, *when* we want."

His expression didn't alter, his eyes steady as he studied her. Then he tilted his head toward the door they stood in front of.

"These are my quarters. Ours now."

When he took a step forward, the door slid open silently. She took a deep breath before she stepped inside. Shit, this was really happening. The quarters were all one room. There was a sitting area to the left of the door with low, wide couches and what looked like an office area with a desk to the right. She couldn't see a kitchen, but an open door behind the sitting area hinted at a bathroom. Her eyes widened. There was only one bed, set on the back wall under a curved window with a stunning space view on the other side. Were they supposed to share it?

He walked past her, shedding his jacket to hang it up near the door to the supposed bathroom. She'd seen him stripped to the waist before, but for a moment her attention was hijacked by the smooth movement of golden satin skin over hard muscle. Shaking her head, she snapped herself out of it.

"So," she said briskly, keeping her tone level and businesslike. "How do we do this?"

He smirked as he turned to face her, his thumbs hooked into his belt. "Do what? Are we having a... what do humans call it... a bird and the insect's conversation? I would have thought you'd have been told that a long time ago."

"What?" She couldn't help the bark of laughter. "You mean the birds and the bees? No... yes! I know about that. I meant the sleeping arrangements. You —" She paused for a moment, lifting her chin. "Surely you don't expect me to sleep in the same bed as you right away?"

His expression was unreadable. Then he spoke, his voice low and measured.

"Much as I would like nothing more than to hold you in my arms as we sleep, I am a red-blooded male with all the usual needs and urges. It would be too much to hold you and not touch you."

He stepped forward, invading her personal space to pull her closer. She stiffened in his arms, the dress uniform looped over her arm held between them like a shield. She wouldn't make a fool of herself again at his touch.

"You'll sleep better without me in here, but I won't be far away if you need me. Sweet dreams, *kelarris,*" he murmured, dropping a kiss on her forehead.

Then he stepped back, triggering the doors, and left her on her own.

7

Kissing Dani was like nothing else. She'd been so tiny and delicate against him, her lips soft and warm as he'd claimed them. And when she'd kissed him back... Sardaan bit back his growl as he walked through the large double doors into the training area, putting such tempting thoughts to the back of his mind.

He felt on top of the world. Several in fact. Even though he'd spent the night on a thin, hard bunk in the barracks rather than the nice comfortable bed his rank as one of the senior warriors aboard afforded him, he didn't care. It had been well worth it knowing that Dani—*his female*—slept comfortably there instead.

His sleep might not have been the best, but he

was wide awake and totally rejuvenated at the thought of the day ahead. So he walked with pride, as a newly mated male should, with his chin held high, his shoulders back and his chest thrust out.

He didn't mind that they hadn't consummated their mating yet. That would come. In time. He was confident that Dani would yield to him, be happy to accept him into her bed. Maybe, if the goddess favored them, they might even have offspring, like Lord Healer Laarn and his human lady.

"Hey, hey! Look who it is!" a voice called from the other side of the room. "If it isn't the hero of the hour."

He grinned as Riis detached himself from the group already gathered there and strode toward him. Automatically he held out his hand, palm up, as Riis slapped his own into it in the traditional warrior's greeting.

The younger man's eyes were bright with curiosity. "So, how did your first night go? She hasn't killed you yet, so your ugly mug obviously didn't put her off that much."

Sardaan's laugh was deep and genuine. He and Riis had been friends for years and he was used to the male's teasing. "Well, you know what they say about women..."

"No, what do they say about women?"

"Tell us!"

He looked up as he was surrounded by males, all with eager faces as they waited for his answer. They were the youngest and lowliest on the ship. Sons of lower ranked families or the not-so-fortunate younger sons that no one bothered with. Apart from him and Riis.

"They prefer the more mature male, shall we say? One with experience," he drawled, casting a pointed glance at Riis. The younger warrior huffed, folding his arms.

"Yeah... as long as that male isn't in his dotage. Females need stamina as well, to be assured that their male can provide for their... *every* need." He waggled his eyebrows comically.

"Yeah, yeah... like you'd know. Right," Sardaan barked. "Are we here to train, or what?"

He didn't need to order them twice, the youngsters scurrying to partner up and find a training circle. They started to spar, and he walked around the circles, correcting a guard here or demonstrating a particular move there.

While he kept his attention on the youngsters, his mind was free to wander. And wander it did, back to his strategy to win Dani's heart. She was a strong female, not easily manipulated. If he wanted the relationship between them to work, he had to make sure she knew he was sincere.

A sudden lapse in concentration from the circles in front of him warned him they had company. Turning, he saw Dani and Kenna, the human female with the emperor's group, walking into the training hall. Both were outfitted for training.

"Draanth, they're so small..."

"...Are they fully grown?"

"They're not seriously going to fight. Are they?"

"Concentrate on your own bouts," he roared, stepping into the nearest circle to cuff the two fighters upside their ears. If they were so easily distracted, they wouldn't survive their first real battle. Instantly, they all returned their attention to what they were supposed to be doing, sneaking glances at the two females across the hall instead of outright staring.

Sardaan knew what they were all doing. Mainly because his own gaze slid sideways even though he tried to control it. He couldn't help it, his curiosity getting the better of him. Despite the fact he'd fought Dani last night, he couldn't wait to see her in action... when he wasn't trying to defend himself against her.

. . .

SHE WAS NOT GOING to fall in love with an alien, no matter how sexy.

Dani kept her focus locked on her opponent as the two women limbered up. The fact that Kenna had kept up her training while staying with the Lathar was obvious. She moved with a grace and elegance that betrayed her abilities as either a dancer or a fighter, but she wasn't overly muscle bound. Instead, she had a sleek, toned appearance that didn't fool Dani for a moment.

"So, how's the blushing bride feeling this morning?" Kenna smirked as they faced off against each other in one of the circles painted on the floor. If Dani hadn't known what they were for, she might have mistaken them for merely a design in the flooring. The marine rolled her shoulder, the overhead lighting glinting off her necklace. Octagonal tabs hung off a chain. Dani had noticed most of the Latharians wearing them. Like dog tags. "Good wedding night was it?"

"Screw you, Reynolds," she threw back and brought her guard up. "How's it going with you and blondie?"

"It's Xaandril. And none of your business."

The marine moved like lightning, a flurry of exploratory jabs and kicks designed to test Dani's defenses on that side. She had the advantage. She'd seen Dani fight, twice, whereas Dani was operating in the dark where Kenna was concerned. She was a marine, though, and by the looks of the way she moved, a shit-hot one. Assuming she was as tough as coffin nails was a given.

She launched a few testing combinations of her own, kicking off her front leg as she tested Kenna's reactions. As she expected, the other woman's guard was rock solid. They moved around each other, pacing, testing and going back to circling. All the while looking for an opening, the smallest hint of a chink in their opponent's armor.

Even though she kept her attention on Kenna, Dani couldn't help but be aware of the large form of her alien "husband" across the hall. He was barking orders at men fighting each other in circles like the one she and Kenna were in—the Latharian version of a fight ring.

She had no idea where he'd gone last night after leaving her in his quarters. At first, she hadn't believed he'd really gone and had showered with one eye on the door, figuring out at the same time that alien showers worked the same as human ones.

Same with the toilets. After hours of restless tossing and turning, jerking awake at the slightest noise, she'd figured out that no, he wasn't coming back. She finally allowed herself to slide into a restless slumber.

"At least you got one of the good ones."

Kenna's comment, delivered just after a double hook, backhand combination that Dani alternately ducked and blocked, made her raise an eyebrow. "Good ones? What do you mean?"

The other woman somehow managed to launch a vicious three-punch combination attack and jerk her head toward the tall warrior over on the other side of the room at the same time. "Your hubby... those kids he's training? They're the Lathar version of cannon fodder. Younger sons, kids from less affluent families. No one else bothers with them because they're just sent into battle to make up the numbers... they're meant to die."

Dani had to stop her jaw dropping as she blocked a punch. As soon as she was able, she slid a quick glance over to where Sardaan was walking a younger warrior through a fight move. "That doesn't make sense... Not to bother with them, I mean. They'd be far more effective if they were trained well. Fewer casualties that way."

Kenna nodded. "You and I know that, but for all their technology, the Lathar can be very backward in other ways."

"How so?"

Dani moved sharply to the side, switching up her fighting style to see if she could draw Kenna in and then take her to the floor. She and Kenna were a similar height, so, unlike when she had been fighting Sardaan last night, she didn't need to worry about being overpowered easily.

"They operate in a clan or family-based structure rather than the military one we know. Feudalistic almost. Challenge fights and sometimes outright assassination are viable methods of career advancement here."

Dani's eyebrows winged up to almost disappear under her hairline. "Assassination? I thought they were all about honor?"

"Yeah, but they're also all about not getting caught as well." Kenna grinned, a flick of her gaze down saying she'd spotted the slight drop of Dani's guard on the left side. It was a deliberate ploy, but, as Dani had expected, the marine was too experienced to fall for it. Instead, she went for Dani's right knee, which she'd been leaning a little too much weight on.

She moved, launching her attack like a speeding bullet, but Dani was ready for her. With a grunt, she twisted, half taking the impact as Kenna barreled into her. She twisted as they fell, heaving herself up and around. By the time they hit the floor, she had her thighs around the other woman's neck in a brutal headlock.

Kenna didn't give up though, twisting and bucking to try and get Dani off, but she held on, knowing her opponent couldn't hold out long. Sure enough, within seconds Kenna slumped to the floor and then reached a hand out to tap the floor.

"You fight well," Dani complimented her as she unhooked her legs and rolled away. The marine had totally missed the soft movement as Dani lifted the strange octagonal dog-tag from around her neck, pocketing it in a piece of sleight of hand she had learned long before she joined the service. A graceful movement took her to her feet and she held out her hand to help Kenna up. The marine smiled, a little ruefully, as she hauled herself upright and brushed herself down.

"Thanks. Not been beaten *quite* so quickly by another human for months though. I obviously need to train more."

She gave a little smile, about to add a comment

about Kenna not being around many other humans for months, when there was a frustrated growl from the other side of the hall.

"For the goddess' sake, how the draanth do you expect to survive your first battle if you all get so distracted by two females?"

The two women turned to see Sardaan glaring in frustration at the small group of youths. All of whom were very shame-faced and guilty as they looked at their feet or at a point somewhere over the big warrior's shoulder.

"I'm trying to give you tools so you don't end up as an afterthought in some war commander's list of casualties," he raged on, his movements jerky and body tight. "And all you can do is giggle and watch a fight that's nothing to do with you!"

That he cared was obvious, and heat spread out from the center of Dani's chest. Such caring and need to help others in a less fortunate position than himself... it spoke to her on levels she didn't want to admit. Really didn't want to admit.

She exchanged a glance with Kenna and then called out. "Would you like to come and join us?"

The swift look she got from Sardaan was unreadable, but she carried on anyway. Most of the warriors were still youths and smaller than full grown warriors. She wasn't sure how old they were, but some looked to be as young as fourteen or fifteen. Certainly not old enough or physically mature enough to take on adult male warriors.

"We can show you a few human moves that you might not have seen before."

"We don't need no human moves," one muttered, but the group as a whole had started to drift their way. Some cast pleading eyes toward Sardaan as if waiting for permission.

"Oh, you lot might not need human moves," he said. "But perhaps Konaat could have done with some last night. Go on. Perhaps they can teach you something I can't."

There was whooping and within seconds Dani and Kenna found themselves surrounded by a group of Latharian teenagers eager to learn. For the next hour, Dani worked opposite to Kenna, showing the youngsters different moves to utilize their smaller size and agility against bigger opponents, only stopping when a bell sounded.

"Second watch," Sardaan called from the sidelines as the boys all broke away from their opponents and raced across the other side of the hall to collect their belongings. "Change and report to your duty stations as quickly as you can. Don't dawdle or you'll get written up and I can't do trallshit to help you then!"

"I'll go hurry them along," the older warrior who'd been training them with Sardaan when she'd arrived commented, nodding toward Dani as he left.

"That's me as well," said Kenna. "Got some training with Daaynal later. Want to make sure I grab something to eat beforehand. Catch you on the flip side." She saluted and hurried out of the door after the rest.

Leaving Dani alone. With her new alien husband.

"Thank you for your help with them." He walked toward her, stopping a half step away to look down at her. "How did you sleep?"

Heat crawled through her at his nearness, her body tense with anticipation. Carefully taking a step back, she put some distance between them. "I slept well, thank you. And you're more than welcome. They're a nice bunch of lads. Kenna says they're overlooked for training though?"

She deliberately tried to keep the conversation light and on subjects other than their sleeping arrangements. The quirk of his lips said he knew what she was trying to do.

"Unfortunately so. Riis and I are trying to help,

as much as we can. Some of those boys couldn't hold a damn blade the right way when we started."

"You've done well with them."

Reaching for the towel and water bottle she'd left by the wall, she straightened up to find him right there. She gasped and stepped away, but her back collided with the wall. He didn't give her a chance to get away, large hands either side of her shoulders.

"I didn't... sleep," he told her, his voice low and rough. His blue eyes were dark with a heat and desire that took her breath away. "All I could think of was you in my bed. Naked. And that I wanted to be in there with you."

She lifted her chin in challenge, trying to ignore the shiver that swept over her skin. Her entire body prickled, aware of his closeness. He was so close she'd only have to press forward a little and they'd be touching from chest to hips. She tensed, fighting down the temptation to do just that.

"Why you?" The question was out before she could stop it, and he frowned.

"Why me what?"

She needed to keep him talking. If she kept him talking, she could perhaps forget about that kiss last night, the way he'd been a gentleman and given up his bed for her... forget his kindness to the boys everyone else had written off as cannon fodder.

"You said they... by they, I figure you meant the emperor and your leaders, had rigged last night so that I would be claimed by one of your warriors. Forgetting for a moment the diplomatic incident that's likely to have caused... why did they pick you to be my escort? I assume you had standing orders to try and seduce me anyway."

His expression set, and she caught a glimpse of anger in the backs of his eyes. Fleeting, but not at her. At least, she didn't think so.

"Yes. I had orders. But..." He reached out to brush a soft thumb over her cheek. "I'd have done my damnedest to seduce you anyway, orders or no orders."

"You would have?" Someone had stolen her voice, replacing it with the sexy, breathy voice of a sex goddess, or a phone sex worker. "Why?"

He blinked. "You're asking me that?"

"Yes." She met him look for look. Unblinking. "I'm asking. Why were you going to try anyway? Am I some sort of trophy... an easy fuck because you have no women?"

That was the worse-case scenario she could think of. To be wanted purely because of a lack of holes to fuck. Crude, but the truth of it when they got down to brass tacks.

"Seriously?" He barked a laugh, pushing off the wall to run a hand through his hair. He looked down at her, an incredulous look in his eyes. "You think... *draanth,* if I was just looking for something soft to fuck, I'd head to one of the pleasure houses. There are plenty of species in the galaxy with compatible genitals to the Lathar. I don't need to try and seduce a reluctant bloody human just for somewhere to stick my cock!"

8
---

*S*he needed to get off this damn ship and the quicker the better.

After their little altercation in the training hall, Sardaan had stormed off, leaving Dani all on her own. She didn't mind, wanting to be anywhere but where the tall, pissed-off Latharian warrior was.

She bit her lip as she looked at herself in the mirror. The only place she felt she could really let her guard down was in the small bathroom off Sardaan's quarters. She wouldn't put it past them to have bugged his room, especially since this had apparently been a setup from start to finish, but she seriously doubted they'd gone as far as bugging his washroom. At least, she really hoped they wouldn't be that indelicate.

She'd made him mad. Running a hand through her hair, she sighed. Sure, she'd made lots of people mad over the years. Couldn't make a cake without breaking some eggs, and she'd broken more than a few people's moods when she'd risen through the ranks to major general. Even more when she'd won the All-Trial year after year.

And she'd rather be back there, on the start line, knowing most of the people around her were going to try and kill her or otherwise knock her out of the running over the following seven days than face Sardaan's furious expression again.

He'd been going to try and seduce her. But why? *Because he'd wanted to,* the little voice in her head shot back. Forget the delicate diplomatic situation between their species... he'd planned to seduce her because he wanted her. That, and the emotion in the backs of his eyes, scared the shit out of her more than the possibility of a full-scale war.

She had to get out of here. Before she did something stupid... like fall in love with her own husband.

Pushing off from the vanity, she shoved her hands through her hair, slicking it back off her face.

"Okay, Dani," she told herself, bolstering her

nerve. "You got this. Walk in the park compared to the All-Trial."

Getting out of Sardaan's quarters was a piece of cake. She had Kenna's octagonal dog tags to get her through doors. She'd felt a little bad for stealing from the other woman, but all was fair in love and war... and it was obvious which side Kenna had thrown her lot in with.

As soon as she left the quarters, Dani turned left and started to follow the path she'd memorized from the hall and shuttle bay last night. It wasn't a long walk, but she'd be alone and in an area she shouldn't be in. Any Lathar who saw her would know she was up to something. Then the game would be up quicker than she could blink.

Reaching the corner, she ignored the heavy bass of her heart and the sweat sliding down the center of her back. The next section was guarded by those damn combat bots. And if just one of those saw her... she was fucked. Big time. They moved too quickly for her to get away and unlike an alien warrior, who she *might* have had a chance against, there was no way she could fight one.

Holding her breath, she peeked around the corner. One quick look, a snapshot of the corridor and she ducked back. The bots were all still in their alcoves. Shit. She couldn't even tell which one was active. They all looked dormant.

Heart in her throat and her stomach in knots, she crept forward. As a serving soldier danger was nothing new to her... but this was something else entirely. There was something about the bots that crept into her brain and triggered primal survival instincts.

The last time she'd been so close to outright terror had been on E-seven-B-four, one of the outer planets in the Esphen system. The whole planet was riddled with vampire spiders the size of small dogs. Needless to say, they hadn't spent long dirt-side, just long enough to rescue the surviving crew of an ill-fated outpost, but the few hours down there had been enough for a lifetime. *Several* lifetimes.

She slipped from cover. Each rustle of her clothes as she crept forward sounded too loud, like the volume of reality was cranked all the way up and at any moment, she expected the bots in front of her to power up and leap into action. The corridor was pale, almost white. It would show up blood really well...

She put the thought from her mind. Cold sweat

rolled in heavy, fat beads down her spine. Her arms and legs shook, heart going like one of the old freight trains they'd used back home to ferry the ore from the center of the asteroid. She hadn't wanted to be a miner. That's why she'd joined the military... But right about now, she'd take a lifetime never seeing daylight if she could just get past these killer robots without being noticed.

She made it to the middle of the corridor, eyes on stalks as she watched for any of their "eyes" to activate. Sardaan had said there was always a pilot on standby, running diagnostics, but he hadn't said whether there was one per corridor, or if the pilots watched a couple of corridors each.

Hopefully it was the latter, which meant she had a fighting chance of getting past before the pilot cycled through the bots to look at this corridor again.

Three quarters of the way down the corridor, the end was almost in sight. She allowed herself a small sigh of relief, then...

Squeak!

She froze as her boot caught against the flooring, the sound almost deafening. With a gasp, she threw herself forward, going from a standstill to a sprint as she tried to reach the end of the corridor and cover before any of the bots woke. Heart pounding and lungs about fit to burst, she reached the turn and threw herself around it, expecting the corridor to be filled at any second with the death machines and their lethal spinning blades.

It took her a few moments to work out that the thundering noise wasn't the sound of the bots chasing her as she'd expected but the sound of her own heart in her ears. Dragging in a ragged breath, she forced herself to calm down and walked quickly along the corridor toward the hall.

The place was deserted, all the doors open between the corridors, the antechambers and the hall to reveal a cavernous place. It reminded her of a modular building where all the walls could be pulled back and reconfigured to create different spaces. An image of the entire center of the Latharian vessel opened up and occupied with troops filled her mind.

She shivered.

If they did that, and landed on Earth, humanity was done for. Well and truly.

Keeping to the walls, she scooted through the hall quickly, emerging onto the other side and taking the right turn she remembered leading to the shuttle bay. Her own shuttle would have returned to the *Defiant* with Vice President Cole, but the Lathar were just bigger versions of humanity, so she *should* be able to fly one of theirs.

Should. If she could reach the pedals.

She stepped out of cover and into the next corridor when a slight sound alerted her to the fact she was about to have company. With a gasp, she scuttled backward, concealing herself inside one of the rooms off the corridor.

Just in time.

A small group of Latharian warriors marched up the corridor, their crisp movements warning her that these were well trained and dangerous, nothing like the boys she'd helped train this morning.

"*Shit, shit, shit...*" she murmured to herself, risking a glance when the sound of booted footsteps grew fainter. The longer she took, the higher the risk of being caught. She needed to get off this damn ship and fast.

Her luck held, and the corridors between her and the shuttle bay remained empty. Relief hit her as she reached it, the door sliding shut behind her.

Then her eyes widened as she looked at the shuttles in front of her. Only they weren't shuttles. Some were nearly as big as the *Defiant* itself, definitely too big to qualify as shuttles. How the hell did they get them to take off from in here?

Confident she was alone now, she ran past them, and past huge, blocky troop transporters, until she found a section nearer the back with smaller vessels. A smile curved her lips as she spotted a sleek flyer.

"Come to momma," she whispered, ducking under the wing and slapping her stolen tag against the plate at the side of the door. It opened with a whoosh and she clambered inside, almost tripping over her own feet in her rush to get to the pilot's seat.

She fell into it, waving a hand over the panel to activate the pilot's console. Freedom was just a short flight away. Now how did she start the engines on this thing, and then she'd need to open the doors—

The sound of a deep, familiar voice made her freeze, hands motionless in mid-air.

"Hello, darling *wife*," Sardaan said silkily. "Going somewhere?"

Dani turned slowly to find the Latharian warrior watching her. Her heart leaped into her throat at the sight of him sitting in one of the crew seats behind the cockpit. Every line and muscle in his body was tense, his expression hard as he captured her gaze with his.

Oh shit, he was *pissed*.

"Okay, just how much trouble am I in?" she asked with a smile, trying to make a joke of it as she flicked a glance at the door behind him. Perhaps she could get away and find a different shuttle.

"You'll never make it," he warned her in a low voice. "But please, try it anyway."

Her hand strayed toward the console behind her and he smiled. "Controls are all locked out, sweetheart. Did you really think, with all the trouble we went to getting you here, we'd let you go quite so easily?"

Checkmate. She had no moves left—none she could see anyway. She lifted her chin, meeting him look for look. "No. I didn't expect you to. But surely you can understand why I had to try?"

He didn't speak, the silence stretching out between them. She kept herself still through the force of will, iron control over her body. Tension mounted in the air between them, white hot and electric.

"You asked for time," he rasped finally, his expression still as hard as steel. "And I was stupid enough to agree. I thought a little leeway... a little *understanding* on my part would ease the way for us as a mated pair... would set us up for a happy life together."

He levered himself up to stand, the movement graceful and lethal. He stalked toward her. Expression controlled and dangerous. Her heart slammed against the inside of her ribcage as he crowded her against the pilot's console. Fighting the instinct to run, she held her ground.

"But I was a *draanthing* idiot. Wasn't I, sweetheart?" he demanded, his tone soft.

He hadn't snarled or shown anger, and that scared her on a level she hadn't believed possible. Not that he'd hurt her... she didn't think he would and besides, the threat of physical violence, even death, didn't faze her. She'd faced it too often on a battlefield. That was a fear she *knew* how to deal with.

This cold fury though... the awareness between them. His hand as he hooked it around her waist and dragged her forward against him... they all scared the very breath out of her lungs.

His eyes glittered as he looked down at her. "Because you were planning to leave me all along. Weren't you?"

"*No,*" she breathed, hands spread over his broad chest to try and keep some distance between them. "Well... yes, but not because—" She shook her head. "It wasn't like that. You're sweet—"

"*Sweet?*" His low snarl cut her off, the fury ramping up in his eyes again. "And look where that got me. A female who decided to use that against me and run. Well, *wife*, sweet just disappeared."

His gaze latched on to her mouth and she gasped a second before his mouth crashed down over hers. He took advantage of her surprise, prying her lips apart with a hard sweep of his tongue and then thrusting inside.

Fighting him off wasn't an option. His free hand gripped the back of her neck, holding her still as he plundered her lips while the hard arm around her waist kept her captive against his larger body.

She tried to hold herself still against his onslaught. Tried not to respond in any way. She'd survived torture. She could survive this. No problem. Even though he was angry, even though every sensible instinct she had told her to remain rigid, her body started to weaken against his.

She whimpered, as much in frustration with herself as in surrender as she slid her hands up his chest. Not holding him close, but not pushing him away either. He rumbled in the back of his throat, pulling her even closer. His tongue swept against hers and she caught her breath, fighting the urge to respond to him.

He pulled away, his lips hovering just against hers. When her breath caught in a small sound of disappointment, she felt his lips curve against hers. "Seems you're fighting yourself as much as me, *kelarris*."

9

His lips covered hers again and Dani was lost. Her body relaxed against his as the world around them fell away, leaving just the two of them locked in a close embrace.

His lips stroked hers, gentler this time, and she moaned, following them as they moved over hers. She forgot why this was such a bad idea. Why fight what felt so good? Why argue when she could be kissing him instead?

With a soft moan, she did just that, parting her lips to kiss him back. He groaned in the back of his throat, his arms tightening around her. Lifting her as they kissed, he boosted her up to sit on the console, the chatter of the computer systems behind them ignored. He nudged her legs apart with a hard thigh, settling between them as he eased her lips apart again.

This time he didn't have to use force. She opened for him immediately, desperate for more of his kisses. This... she'd known this was coming from the first moment they'd met. She'd sensed the tension, the spark, between them and wanted more.

Lifting her hands, she drove them into the hair that fell to cover his shoulders, pressing herself flush against him. He nipped her lower lip in reply, teasing her with hot, open-mouthed kisses that ramped the tension between them to inferno level.

His hand, large and warm, covered the back of her hips, and he yanked her forward until he pressed against her... right where she needed him most. A gasp escaped her, lost in his mouth, as the thick length of his cock pressed into her.

Fuck, he was huge. A shiver of nerves swept through her, but his next kiss, deep and passionate, stole her ability to think. Instead, driven by instinct she just reacted, hands smoothing over his shoulders to hold him to her. She wanted this. Needed this. Needed to feel his bigger, harder body moving against hers.

He seemed affected by the same madness, pulling at the hem of her top. She lifted her arms so he could yank it up over her head. He looked down at her for a moment, eyes glittering in the semi-darkness, the wash of the console lights illuminating the tightness of his features.

She bit her lip, watching his expression. Her plain bra wasn't the sexiest thing out there and her figure was sparse due to years of training...

He whispered something in Latharian she didn't understand, but his expression and the sudden heat in his eyes meant she didn't need to. Cupping her cheeks, he swept his hands down her neck and then down her arms.

She shivered as his hands encircled her wrists for a second, the movement highlighting how much bigger and stronger they were compared to hers. Then they were back, sweeping up the sides of her waist and ribcage, arching her backward as he bent over her.

Her breathing caught as his hair brushed the soft skin of her cleavage, her entire body tight with anticipation. His lips brushed her skin in feather light caresses, like butterflies brushing against her. But butterflies that left a trail of fire in their wake.

She clung to him, her hands driving into his hair as he worked his way down the center of her cleavage and then out, kissing along the line of satin.

Her nipples beaded, hard peaks that scratched against the inside of the formerly soft cups, desperate for his attention.

He moved, and her bra was gone, sliding down her arms and discarded as he looked down at her.

"Beautiful," he murmured and bent his head again.

She bit back her moan as he captured a nipple between his lips, pulling it into the hot cavern of his mouth. He didn't kiss. He tormented. Sucked and licked at the stiff bud until heat rolled through her body and her pussy clenched. Dizzy with arousal, she couldn't help the rock of her hips against him. The movement pressed her aching clit against the stiff bar of his cock and he growled. Then he sucked harder.

She cried out, the soft, feminine sound loud in the quiet confines of the shuttle. They were alone, but she wouldn't have cared anyway, locked in the spell he'd woven around her.

"Mine," he growled against her skin, nipping her nipple gently. She gasped, a bolt of pleasure arrowing from the stiff bud straight down to her clit. "And I *will* have you."

She didn't put up a fight as he pushed her back down against the cool surface of the console and reached for her belt. Her limbs were weak, heat consuming her as he unsnapped her combats, yanking them down over her hips and lower. He discarded them with her boots on the floor behind him.

Then he was back, shedding his own shirt as he looked down at her clad only in the tiniest of panties. The same heat that rolled through her was reflected in his eyes. She arched her back, hands in her hair, an instinctive move to display her body better for him.

He smiled in approval, the expression tight, and slid a big hand up one of her thighs. Strong fingers tangled in her panties and, before she realized what he was doing, he yanked them clean off her.

Her gasp was soft and filled with arousal. She'd never had a guy who wanted her so much that he literally ripped the clothes from her body. But the small sound was drowned out by his growl as he looked at her in all her naked glory.

"I want…" he didn't seem able to put the rest of the thought into words and reached for her instead.

One hand slammed into the console by her head, his lips covering hers at the same moment strong fingers slid through her pussy lips. A strangled cry escaped her as pure pleasure shot through her system.

If she'd been able to think before, she certainly couldn't now, as her handsome warrior played her responses like a master musician with his favorite instrument. She whimpered, gasped and shuddered as he drove her higher and higher to the peak of pleasure. Each stroke, flick or circle was seemingly designed for maximum effect.

She kissed him back, clinging to his strong arms to urge him on, and then... in a blinding moment of clarity, ecstasy exploded through her. Her cry was more a scream as her body became a battlefield of heat, need and pleasure. It shattered her, broke her bone from bone, cell from cell, and made her anew.

Strong arms closed around her as he dragged her upright, holding her against him. He stroked her through her release. Dragged it out until she lay pliant and shuddering in his arms, her body racked by aftershocks.

"You are..." he murmured, his voice a deep rasp. "Ut—"

"*Sardaan? You in there?*" a voice called outside.

Dani started, drawing closer to Sardaan's bigger

form as a figure appeared in the shuttle hatch for a moment.

"Oh *draanth,* sorry. Sardaan, we need you. Aariin is hurt. Bad."

OH MY GOD, that had really just happened.

Heat hit Dani's cheeks, burning the skin like she'd spent too long out in the sun as she hastily pulled her clothes on. Her panties were ruined so she shoved them in her pants pocket. Sardaan's deep voice outside the shuttle reached her ears. He was asking questions about Aariin, his tone rising with tension.

She shoved a shaking hand through her hair and then bent over to pull her boots on. How the hell had she gone from escaping to... shit, she'd practically given it up to him right there in the damn cockpit. What had happened to cool and collected?

"Dani. Either you're done now, or you're walking to the medbay half-naked," Sardaan called from outside the shuttle. She took a second to smooth her clothes down before stepping through the hatch.

"I'm good," she murmured, not quite meeting his eyes as his hand latched around her wrist. She was his prisoner now, even more so than she had been before.

He flicked her a glance, nodding curtly. "Come on."

By the time they reached the medbay, the healers were already there and working on Aariin. Dani recognized him instantly as one of the teenagers she'd helped train that morning. Where he'd been lively and chatty earlier, though, now he was pale as he lay on the bed, his skin gray and his eyes unfocused as he stared up at the ceiling. He blinked slowly, still alive, but she'd seen enough injured soldiers to know it wasn't good.

Staying to the side, she wrapped her arms around herself and stayed out of the way as the healers worked. Now they'd stopped moving, and she was surplus to requirements, emotion hit her hard and fast as her brain tried to process what had happened.

She'd given in to him. She ran her hand through her hair, her cheeks heating. After all her pretty words to herself about not falling for the handsome alien warrior, she recognized her headlong flight to escape for what it was. *Running scared.* She'd known if she stayed around she wouldn't be able to resist. And guess what? She hadn't.

All he'd had to do was touch her... kiss her... and her defenses had folded quicker than a damn chocolate teapot. Shivering, she forced the thoughts down and concentrated on what was going on around her.

The medbay was filled to bursting with the group of teenagers and other, older warriors, one of whom was covered in blood. Aariin's blood.

"How's he doing?" Sardaan asked, storming up to the edge of the treatment bay.

From what she could work out, the faint blue shimmer around the bed was some kind of sterile force field, allowing them to turn each bay into an impromptu operating theatre.

"Touch and go. Shut up," Isan grunted, not looking up.

The healer was almost elbow deep in the boy's chest cavity, some kind of gloves over his hands as he worked. Strain showed on his features, but his eyes were sharp and focused.

"What happened?" Sardaan demanded, looking at the shorter warrior next to them. Riis. She'd gleaned his name from Kenna. The boy who come to find them had only been able to tell them Aariin had been hurt while on duty, his voice tight when Sardaan questioned him outside the shuttle as she'd dressed.

"He slipped while fitting a secondary relay, fell from a ladder and knocked Warrior Ter over. Ter took offense and demanded challenge. Aariin—"

"What?" Sardaan's voice sliced through the air like a whip as he turned to look at the blood-covered warrior. "You demanded challenge? From a *Quesen?*"

The other warrior's expression set, eyes hard. "How was I to know he was one of the lowest?"

"Look at them! How could you miss they were *Quesen?*" Sardaan bellowed, sweeping an arm at the group of teenagers gathered to one side of the medbay. Next to the group of adult warriors, it was easy to see that their clothing was secondhand or inferior quality, the same as their weapons. They didn't hold themselves the same as the older warriors either. While they all stood straight, their shoulders back, they didn't quite meet anyone's eyes, their expressions set.

Downtrodden, she realized. No one cared for them and they didn't expect anyone to. Her heart ached, a deep pang near the center of her chest.

Ter shrugged. "He was rude. Honor had to be satisfied. How was I to know he couldn't block a simple Trexian hammer-slice?"

Sardaan stiffened, his expression incredulous. "There's *nothing* simple about any of the Trexian moves, let alone the hammer combinations. *Quesen* aren't trained to that level. *Everyone* knows that!"

"*ENOUGH!*" Isan shouted from within the bay. "If you're going to fight, take it outside. I have enough to deal with here."

He hadn't moved from his position by the bed as he fought to save the boy's life. From the amount of blood, Dani knew the healer had already lost the battle. Lathar were a bigger version of humanity, or humans were a smaller version of Lathar. She didn't know which way around it was, and she didn't care. What she *did* know was that no one could end up with that much blood outside their body and survive.

"We're losing him" the healer murmured, looking around at the healers around him who were monitoring the equipment crammed into the bay. They shook their heads, expressions taut, and her heart sank.

"Sardaan," she murmured to get his attention.

He whirled around, spearing her with a hard look. For a moment she was back in the shuttle, his rage and fury freezing her into place. She swallowed and motioned toward the healer and his patient.

His focus shifted and he was there in an instant. Isan swore, stepping back and tearing the gloves from his hands to shove his hands through his hair.

"He's gone. I can't bring him back."

The words dropped into the sudden silence of the medbay. Sardaan's growl was low and terrible as he spun on his heel, fixing Ter with a gaze so terrible it made even Dani shake down to her soul. It was the kind of look that promised retribution and pain. The sort of look that said no matter what the cost, he would make Ter pay for what he'd done.

"*Nonono*," Riis got in front of Sardaan before he could take a step forward, a hand slammed into the center of the bigger warrior's chest. "Bad move, don't do this." His gaze was intent as he looked at his friend, words low and urgent.

Sardaan looked at him, his eyes empty of everything but fury and retribution for a moment. "He killed Aariin. *Slaughtered* him. Tell me how that doesn't need an answer. Tell me how I can let that slide?"

Dani flitted closer, his pain calling out to her and drawing her in. The need to soothe him overwhelmed her and she reached out warily, but paused halfway at the interchange between the two warriors. Whatever the situation was between them, he was hurting. She couldn't leave him to deal with that alone.

"Not here, not now. You have a mate. Remember?" Riis insisted, his gaze flicking to her for a second. His look plainly said *help me out here.* "She is your first priority."

Shit. She had to do something, or there was going to be a bloodbath in here.

---

10

*F*ury raced through Sardaan's veins, burning away everything he was until all that was left was an inferno of anger, the need for vengeance at its core.

Baring his teeth, he focused on Ter on the other side of the medbay. The piece of *trallshit* had just killed, no... *murdered...* a kid in cold blood, and he was standing there grinning with his clansmen like this was just a day out on the outer rings.

A snarl of rage escaped his lips again and he surged forward, trying to push Riis out of the way. He looked down at the smaller warrior.

"Move. Now."

"Sardaan?" Dani murmured, sliding her hand

around his muscled upper arm. Her soft touch stilled him instantly and he looked down at her. Her dark eyes were filled with concern. "This doesn't help Aariin. Not at the moment. Please?"

He wanted to brush her off, push Riis aside and storm across the room to grab Ter by his throat and shake him until he stopped fucking laughing. How dare he laugh when Aariin lay dead behind them, his body not yet cold? Even as he looked at his concerned mate, gaze locked with hers, his mind raced, the need for vengeance uppermost.

Ter had *known* Aariin couldn't beat him. There was no way the *Quesen*, who had not attained his full growth had either the capability or skill to match Ter, a warrior in his prime.

Frustration rolled through Sardaan at their honor system. One that allowed a warrior such as Ter to challenge a *Quesen*, a warrior so below him in the ranking system it was a joke. The challenge fights weren't designed for that and most warriors would never step into a ring with someone so below them in skill and ability. To do so, knowing it would be a whitewash, was without honor. But it wasn't illegal.

Guilt hit him hard and fast, on the tail end of his

frustration. He should have shown the *Quesen* all the Trexian combinations and their countermoves, how to block and answer them. If he had, as Aariin had asked, the boy might be alive today. Just seeing the counters once might have given the youngster an edge in the battle.

Instead, Ter had cleaved his chest in two.

Sardaan lifted his gaze, breaking away from Dani's to look at Ter. But *he* wasn't a *Quesen*, not anymore, and he certainly *did* know how to block all the fucking Trexian moves and how to retaliate. He'd wipe the floor with Ter, teach him to pick on those smaller and less skilled than he was.

He'd have to kill Ter, though. Just humiliating him as Sardaan wanted to, while satisfying, would be a stupid move. A humiliated enemy—because today Ter had proven himself to be an enemy of the duty and honor Sardaan held dear—was a dangerous enemy. He'd have to watch his back for the rest of his life.

Not just him, he realized, as the small hand on his arm slid upward. He had a mate now, and Ter wouldn't hesitate to use her against him. Or worse, try and claim her for himself. *That* he would never allow to happen.

But Ter wasn't alone. A T'Raniis, Ter had many brothers. Sardaan's eyes narrowed. He'd have to kill them all. *Fuck.* There were just too many of them to make that a viable plan.

Plus, Riis was right. Dani's safety took priority.

"Please. Sardaan..."

He looked back at her. She actually sounded worried about him. Or was she more worried that she'd lose her protection in a society she didn't understand? He knew that if he fell, Riis or one of the others would stand in and protect her, but she didn't—a lapse he would have to rectify and soon.

Reaching out, he hauled her up against him, bending down so his lips whispered over hers. "Because you command it."

Utter *trallshit*. He'd been a hairsbreadth from challenging the arrogant older warrior and they both knew it, but ceding to his mate's wishes gave him an honorable out.

"That's it. You run away and hide behind a female's skirts," Ter shouted from the other side of the medbay as Sardaan turned to go, his arm around Dani's waist. He whirled around, the sudden fury that exploded through him blinding him to the stupidity of killing Ter in front of everyone.

He didn't get the chance. Instead, Isan stepped

between them, his expression forbidding as he turned toward Ter. Still covered in blood and scarred from head to foot, he was a nightmarish image.

"You're very free and easy with those insults, Ter T'Raniis," the healer said, his voice tight and controlled as fury blazed in his eyes. "How about you throw them at *me* and see where you get?"

Ter's skin paled and he took a step backward, dropping his gaze. Sardaan hadn't expected anything else. No one wanted a healer pissed at them. Unlike what he'd seen of humanity's doctors, who took a vow not to hurt anyone, Latharian healers were experienced and deadly warriors. None more so than Isan, who, along with his scars, had more braids than Ter and his companions put together.

"No," Isan growled, contempt in his voice. "Get the fuck out of my medbay. *Now.*"

"Yes, Healer. Right away."

As one, Ter and his buddies beat it out of the other door of the medical bay, not one of them daring a look back at either Isan nor Sardaan and the group of *Quesen*. Once they'd gone, the healer turned to them.

"We will prepare Aariin for the final rites," he said quietly, his expression drawn. Sardaan had known Isan from when they were boys, and he knew the loss of a patient, any patient, weighed heavily on him. "He will be laid out in honor in the smaller hall of the Lady Goddess."

Sardaan inclined his head. "Thank you. I will inform his duty commander and his family."

SARDAAN WAS HURTING. Anyone could see that. Dani bit her lip, wanting nothing more than to take that pain away. She knew what it was like to lose people. She'd lost more men than she'd ever wanted to count, and that letter or call home never got any easier. She remembered each and every one, their names and dates of death inscribed in her memory, where they would stay until the day she died.

She knew the pain and wished she could take it away from him.

With gentle hands, she pulled him back around and urged him toward the doorway. Her gaze locked with Riis', and even though they were human and Lathar, from different planets and backgrounds, they moved as one. Dani ushered Sardaan out of the medical bay and Riis ushered the small group of boys out.

"Where wil—"

"I'll speak to their duty commanders," Riis cut her off, his voice firm. "Get them some compassionate leave. At least until the rites for Aariin. You..." he looked at Sardaan, the big warrior glowering as a tiny muscle worked in his jaw. "Look after your mate," he ordered, although she wasn't sure whether that was directed at her or Sardaan.

She nodded anyway, tucking herself in against her alien husband's side and patting his chest gently. "I can't remember which way back to our quarters," she said softly, pulling his attention to her as Riis led the teenagers away, their shoulders slumped like dejected ducklings as they trailed after him.

Sardaan's gaze cut to her, the expression in his eyes cold and hard. "No? Sure about that? Because you sure as *trall* could find your way from them to the shuttle bay. Couldn't you?"

She froze, rooted to the spot as he pinned her with his gaze. Anger radiated from his tense shoulders, the free hand not around her waist clenched into a tight fist.

"About that—"

"No!" he snapped, yanking her up hard against his side, feet planted wide. "I don't want to hear excuses. You tried to run. You failed. Deal with the consequences."

"C-consequences?" Her voice gave out on her, the word emerging soft and breathy. Hands spread over his broad chest, she tried to put some distance between them, but it was impossible. Not unless she wanted to break her own back on the steel bar that was his arm around her waist.

"Consequences," he repeated, his nostrils flaring. "Time's up. You're mine."

Her breathing caught on a tiny hitch as he bent and scooped her up into his arms. At the look on his face, she didn't dare argue. This was not some fellow soldier she could reach on the level of a colleague, or use the chain of command with.

He was something else. Her... mate. Her brain latched onto the alien term as the only one that fit their current situation as he strode through the corridors. The tension between them grew the closer they got to his quarters, almost at breaking point by the time he stalked through them.

As soon as they were inside the room, the doors swept shut. He barked a command in Latharian she didn't understand, dropping her feet to the floor and backing her up against the now closed doors in the same second.

Heat hit her broadside, a fluttering in the pit of her stomach stealing her breath. He crowded her, his bigger body hot and hard against hers as her back pressed against the cold metal of the door.

"Mine," he growled again and kissed her.

It wasn't a kiss though. Not *just* a kiss. Instead, it was an angry declaration of ownership... an order for her surrender... and a demand for her submission all rolled into one.

She whimpered, the sound lost under his lips, and gave him what she knew he needed. Her body relaxed against his, her lips parting in surrender. He paused, just for a second, and then growled again in the back of his throat. One big hand cupped the side of her neck, sliding up to cradle the back of her head as he ravished her mouth with his.

The hard thrust of his tongue, the utterly dominant way he kissed her... like he owned her... triggered responses she didn't realize she had. With the softest murmur, she wrapped herself around him, struggling to remember why this wasn't exactly what she wanted.

It was exactly what she needed.

Every cell in her body clamored for her to get closer to him. To wrap herself around him and kiss him back in a torrent of heat and need that swept everything else away. The release he'd brought her to in the shuttle teased her now, her body wound tighter than a spring.

He groaned, the sound deep in his chest as he registered the change. Pulling her away from the door slightly, he yanked her top off again, her bra gone in a heartbeat. His mouth crashed down over hers again, in hot, open-mouthed kisses only interrupted as he stripped her combats and boots from her. She shivered as she stood there, completely nude, but just as quickly he was back, crowding her against the door again.

A moan escaped her lips as he boosted her up. His hands were hard on her hips, under her ass to support her as he ground his leather-clad crotch against her. The fact he was almost fully dressed sent her arousal higher than she'd thought possible.

He broke the kiss, looking into her eyes, and for a moment the angry mask slipped.

"Gods, you're so fucking beautiful, *kelarris*." The raspy admission was torn from him and his lips compressed as he reached down between them. He moved, and the thick, hard head of his cock pressed against the entrance to her body.

Her eyes widened. He was just as huge as she'd

thought. There was no way she'd be able to take him.

"Sard—"

His lips over hers cut her off, and he shoved into her. She froze, hands curled around his heavily muscled upper arms as her entire body tensed at the intrusion. He thrust again, forcing her body to part around his, and she gasped, not able to stop his kiss or his penetration. He did it again, body hard and urgent against hers, but all she could focus on was the feel of his thick cock stretching her, of her pussy forced to part around him as he worked his way into her with short, hard thrusts.

Then he was in her completely, his groan in her ear as their hips met low and rough. She closed her eyes, every part of her awareness focused on where they were joined. Her pussy throbbed around his cock, her breathing coming in short pants as she got used to the feeling of him inside her.

One thing was for sure. Latharian men were built *way* bigger.

He pulled back, his expression hard but his gaze intent as he scanned her face. Checking, she realized. Making sure he hadn't hurt her. Even in the midst of his anger, he cared enough to check that he hadn't hurt her.

"*Draanth*," he hissed, a big hand on her ass. "You're so fucking tight."

She didn't answer. Couldn't. The feel of him filling her completely took up all her brain power. He shivered, and the movement made his thick cock slide against her slick inner walls, stroking the nerve endings there. Her head fell back against the door, a soft moan escaping her.

"Again..." she whispered, unable to help herself. She'd pull herself back together tomorrow, but for now... She just wanted him. "Harder."

He growled, free hand snaking up to hook around the back of her neck, and did as she asked. Pulling back, he surged up into her again. Pinned between his hard body and the door, she had nowhere to go... had to accept each hard thrust as he took her. Claimed her against the door.

Heat and need rolled through her, spurred on by each thrust, each deep moan as he slammed into her. She went from anticipating each hard movement to moaning in bliss when it came. He got harder and faster, every muscle in his big, powerful body bent to one end. Taking her.

Rearing back, he flicked his hair back over his shoulder, his face a mask of passion and deep, dark desire as he looked down at her. She saw the decision there before he moved.

"Not here," he grunted, pulling out of her in one quick move. She let out a tiny gasp as her feet hit the floor, clutching at him for balance, but she needn't have worried. In the next second he'd scooped her up in his arms and strode toward the bed.

He dropped her onto the soft surface. Before she'd registered the coolness of the sheets beneath her, he was back inside her. The hard thrust made them both moan.

"*This* was how I imagined you, that first time I saw you," he admitted, braced above her on one elbow as his free hand hauled her knee up against his hip. He hadn't stopped moving, his hips pistoning against hers. He leaned down, his lips whispering the words against hers. "Beneath me, a look of pleasure on your beautiful face as I claimed you for my own. And now you are. Beneath me. *Mine.*"

The look on his face, all masculine determination and dark heat, made her clench around him again. She'd never seen herself as the submissive type, but the thought he'd been so determined to get her did something deep inside.

Conversation ceased as he upped the pace. She

couldn't help but look at him, male beauty defined by desire. His hair swayed against his shoulders, his gaze locked to hers with each strong thrust. Watching the changes in his eyes as he pushed them both higher and closer to the edge was the most erotic thing she'd ever seen. With a soft moan, she wrapped her legs around his hips, moving with him.

"Yours," she whispered, her hands sliding over his shoulders. He growled and caught them with one of his, hauling them above her head to pin them there with one hand.

Normally she'd have fought and squirmed to get free. But not here. Not now. There was something about him, something about the look in his eyes, that reached deep into the part of her that she kept hidden from everyone. The part that wanted to belong. To someone... to something.

Now she realized that something was him.

"Always mine," he rumbled. Holding her down, he sped up. Heat blazed in his eyes as he took her hard and fast, pushing them both up to the edge. Her breath came in short pants, her pussy clenching tightly around his invading cock. Hell, even her toes curled as she silently urged him on. She needed this, needed him, needed more...

Heat exploded through her, her body shattering

as ecstasy hit. Her breathing locked, her pussy clenching hard as her spine arched. She moaned in pleasure, hearing his growl as he sped up. She couldn't help clenching hard around each powerful thrust. His thrusts became erratic until he slammed into her one last time, roaring his pleasure against her neck as he came deep within her.

11

*H*er alien mate was the most handsome man she'd ever seen.

Dani had woken early as usual, her body clock conditioned by years of military service. Tiredness washed through her, so she didn't attempt to get up. She simply lay on her side to study the other occupant of the large bed.

Sardaan lay on his side, asleep. His dirty-silver hair pooled beneath his head, several braids falling into the hollow at the front of his throat. She itched to reach out and touch them. There were so many, woven intricately through his hair on one side, all fastened with small beads or ties.

She tilted her head to look at them. They were all different colors and types... denoting different military engagements maybe, like Terran medal ribbons? She'd have to ask him when he woke up.

Her gaze slid over him, studying him in a way she couldn't while he was awake. In sleep he seemed peaceful, like a slumbering angel. She almost snorted at her fanciful thoughts. If he was an angel, though, he had to be the angel of death or war. She wasn't big on religion, but she was fairly sure several of them had warrior angels. Sardaan, with his long hair and heavily muscled physique would certainly fit the bill. She could just see him in formfitting armor with a sword in one hand and a heavenly bolt or something in the other.

Broad shoulders carved with muscle bracketed a wide chest free of hair, sliding into cobblestone abs. The sheet covered him from the waist down, but her memory filled in the lean hips and muscled rugby-player's thighs. She had no clue if the Lathar played rugby or anything like it, but if they did, Sardaan would fit right in. A flush of heat kissed her cheeks as her memory, and the soreness between her thighs filled in the rest of what was beneath the sheet.

One thing was for sure, Latharians had some serious stamina. She'd had a few passion-filled all-nighters in her time, but last night blew them all out of the water. Insatiable wasn't the word. He'd taken her more times than she could count, from hard and fast to so slow and gentle as they lay spooning on the bed. Just the memory made her shiver.

"Like what you see, *kelarris*?" he asked, making her jump.

He opened his eyes, the odd colors and feline-like pupils bringing it home to her that he wasn't human. Right now, though, his eyes were wide and so dark, they almost looked human.

"How long have you been awake?" she asked, feeling a little self-conscious and shy even though there was no need to be. He'd seen everything about her last night. "And what does that mean... *kelarris*? You called me that before."

"It means 'beloved' in my language." He smiled and reached out to smooth her sleep-rumpled hair back from her face. "And I've been awake long enough to know my mate has been watching me. And you know what?" he asked, stroking his thumb against her lower lip. "I like it. And I like the way you look well loved, as a new mate should."

She blushed. She actually blushed.

"Yeah, well. I wanted to talk to you about that."

His small growl warned her, her gaze flicking up to meet his. "I'm not letting you go, Dani. Not ever."

She hissed in exasperation, trying to yank her

face from his grip. "Oh for heaven's sake, Sardaan. One night is fine, but just look at us... It's never going to work!"

He didn't let go, his grip on her jaw firm as he made her look at him. "Why not? It certainly seemed to be working last night."

She gave in. He was too strong for her to fight, and she favored him with a look. "Yes. You're male. I'm female. We have compatible genitals. But... come on, how old are you? Mid-twenties?" She sighed. "I'm a little bit older than that. And I have a career... duties to get back to."

He blinked and then chuckled. "Is that it? *That's* what you're worried about? The age difference?"

The heat on her cheeks intensified and she nodded. "Well, wouldn't you? I know you guys don't have many women, but there's no need for you to saddle yourself with a woman who'll be old when you're in the prime of your life..." *And she didn't want to see him walk away or choose someone else.*

She ignored the little voice in the back of her head. It might be right, but that didn't mean she had to listen to it.

His hand slid into the back of her neck, strong fingers massaging gently. "Little mate, I'm older than you are, by a few years... and even if I wasn't, I wouldn't care. You're mine. End of story."

She couldn't help the small snort of amusement that escaped. "Older than me? Sure, right. Have you looked in a mirror recently, handsome?"

His lips broke into a smile. "You think I'm handsome? This is good. I like the fact my mate finds me desirable."

She shoved lightly at his broad shoulder as he pulled her closer. "Oh, get over yourself! Seriously Sardaan, I'm forty-two. You're what? Twenty-five?"

"Add another twenty." His expression was amused at her reaction. "We age slower. So will you now. It's a simple genetic patch."

"Patch? You make it sound like mending a fucking blanket!"

"It's about as simple. And I'm done talking," he growled, his eyes darkening as he rolled over and yanked her under him in the same movement. His knee pressed between hers and in the next movement, he was inside her.

"Oh!" she managed, thought processes cut off by the sudden movement. Then her toes curled, and her body wrapped itself around him automatically. Despite all the times he'd taken her the night before, she wanted more. Needed more.

"Didn't put you down as a morning sex type of person," she murmured as he began to move. It was slow and languid, the pleasure of each stroke bubbling through her blood like the fizz in fine champagne.

A moan welled up in the back of her throat, but she held it back. He didn't need his head swelling any further. He didn't need to know she was rapidly becoming addicted to him. Because she was, and it was going to hurt like a fucking bitch when she had to leave.

"I'm an anytime sex kind of male when it comes to you," he said against her ear, the soft brush of his lips against her earlobe as he thrust slowly sending shivers down her spine. "I want you. All the time. Even when I was sleeping, my dreams were of you beneath me, your pretty thighs parted in welcome as I plundered your sweet pussy... or you riding me, impaled on my cock with a look of bliss on your gorgeous face. I wish our races were telepathic so you could see how I see you. How much you fucking turn me on. You're it for me, Dani. For as long as I live."

With each word, his thrusts got harder and faster, until the bed beneath them rocked against the wall again. Her moan escaped. What did her old life have that was better than this? Better than a guy who looked the way he did, crazy about her? Better than a guy from a society that mated for life, no cheating.

Her climax was swift and all consuming. His name was on her lips as she shattered apart around him. He followed her within a few strokes, his cock jerking and pulsing within her to coat her inner walls with his white-hot seed.

They lay together, each breath shared as they recovered from the slow, but intense coupling. He shivered, the movement passed onto her where they were still joined. His gaze locked with hers, reluctance in his eyes as he pulled free of her with a wet pop.

"I have training," he murmured almost by way of apology, and she saw the darkness reenter his eyes as he remembered Aariin.

"Go," she said softly, stroking his jaw. His stubble was significantly heavier this morning and the new information, that Lathar needed to shave just like human men, softened her even more toward him. They weren't so different. Perhaps she could make a life here?

"I'll find you later," he promised. "After training."

~

Was she really about to do this? Ask the Latharian emperor himself for help? Well, not in quite so many words, but that was what it amounted to. She needed his help to figure out a way she could stay here without feeling that she'd betrayed her own people.

Dani shivered as she sat looking around while waiting for the emperor to see her. The room was as opulent as she'd have expected an antechamber in an emperor's suite, with low, plush couches and fine wooden furniture that wouldn't have looked out of place in any ancient palace on Earth. She assumed anyway. A colony brat, she'd never been to one, but she'd seen pictures.

She'd been given a book on princes and princesses when she was a child. She'd loved to look through the pictures of castles and dresses, her childish imagination painting pictures... in her mind she'd been a lost princess, banished to the outer work colonies. Someday her prince would come and take her away from it all, bringing her family along as well. They'd all live in a fancy palace and have tea and cucumber sandwiches.

Then age and reality had intruded. Her parents had been stolen from her by the Sweats that had ripped through the base. A bad vein of aurillium had been opened, a mutated virus decimating the workforce. She'd joined up the same day she'd been old enough, heading off base immediately. Princes be damned. She'd rescue herself, thank you very much.

Now she was married to her own version of a prince. An alien one with silver hair and a sexy smile that melted her heart. She smiled to herself. Not that she'd admit that to Sardaan. His ego would get too big to fit through the door.

A movement over on the other side of the room caught her attention and she looked up to find the emperor's aide watching her. He'd been trying to conceal his interest since she'd arrived. Badly.

He'd been a prick when she'd first arrived, questioning exactly why she wanted to see Daaynal. It seemed secretaries were the same the universe over. This one was just as much a guard dog as any admiral's aide she'd ever met. Perhaps they bred them somewhere and then released them when required.

But this one was more than a guard dog. He was Latharian. Several times she'd caught him looking at her out of the corner of his eye as he sat at the desk, a couple of times without outright heat in his eyes.

Like now. She leveled him a hard look and he looked away quickly.

Sure, she might be human, but she'd happily kick his ass for him. And she was fairly sure if Sardaan knew he'd looked at her that way, he'd come and kick the guy's ass as well. And she *knew* he could. The aide had a decent number of braids, but nowhere near the number Sardaan did.

Pride hit her at the thought. She'd noticed that not many warriors had as many braids as her mate did. Maybe the healer, Isan. She suppressed the cold shiver rolling down her spine. There was something about him that scared even her, and she'd seen an awful lot of scary mofos in her time.

Like that sergeant who'd gone loco during the Devershi campaigns and started collecting "trophies." Ears. Lots of them. He'd killed a couple of officers before they'd caught up to him. She'd been there when the military police had brought him in and she'd never forget the look in his eyes.

Isan wasn't like that, but there was a look in his eyes and an awareness in the way he held himself... she'd rather go toe to toe with the ear-collecting sergeant than face down the healer.

Idly, her gaze wandered over the guy at the desk. She'd noticed that while all the Lathar wore what appeared to be armored leather uniforms, they were all that slight bit different. At first she'd thought perhaps it was because they all purchased according to personal preference, but now she was starting to think it was more than that. None of them wore regimental or unit patches like Terran forces did, but she'd noticed that Sardaan's group wore jackets with double piping and a diamond pattern stitched across the shoulders. The aide in front of her, one of the emperor's group, had a black braid stitched into the shoulder seams of his uniform and vertical stitching. She frowned. Could the design itself be unit based?

"Major General Black?"

The deep voice a few minutes later surprised Dani into looking up from her study of her feet. She'd dressed in the leathers and boots Kenna had given her, Sardaan managing to rustle up a new t-shirt from somewhere. It was a couple of sizes too small, which had made his blue eyes dark with heat, but since she had no other clothes, beggars couldn't be choosers.

As she looked up, she met the steady gaze of the emperor. He watched her with interest and more than a little amusement.

"Or would you three like a little more time alone?" he asked, nodding toward her feet.

Dammit. Her cheeks burned. Bloody soundless Latharian technology. How long had he been standing there?

"Sardaan K'Vass' female does not have an appointment," the aide broke in, shooting a look at her. His pinched expression clearly indicated what he thought about people without appointments. "But she insisted on waiting even though I told her you would be too busy to see her."

He looked at the emperor with a small smile, his expression so smug it was obvious he expected Daaynal to agree with him. "Should I tell her mate to make an appointment for her? I believe you have some free time in a few days..."

He trailed off at the look Daaynal leveled at him. "You're new. Aren't you?"

The man snapped to attention. "Yes, Your Majesty. Newly promoted from the *Keral'Gentar.*"

Daaynal's lips pressed together for a second, his expression unimpressed. "Then you need to get with the times. Human females are far more independent than ours were allowed to be. Major General Black is a leader among her people and I'm sure does not need her mate to speak for her. Am I correct?" he asked Dani, offering his arm.

"Quite," she said, sliding her hand onto the big

warrior-emperor's arm. He was charming, and that in itself was very dangerous. She had a feeling he was used to playing games, but with entire races, rather than just men.

"Good, good," he patted her hand as they walked through the doors into his chambers. "Now, how about you tell me what brings a newly mated beauty like yourself to my door…"

12

*S*he walked into the rooms, her hand still on the large emperor's arm. The slightly old-world formality of the Latharian culture was a little odd, but she was rapidly getting used to it. The luxury of the emperor's apartments didn't disappoint. She swept a gaze around, noting the larger-scale furniture and lush soft furnishings. The emperor obviously liked nice things.

Her gaze scanned the room automatically and she stiffened at the sight of the big combat bot in the corner. Bigger than the ones in the corridor and a different design, it hunkered down like a malevolent metallic spider.

"Don't worry," Daaynal said by her ear. "It's deactivated. Perfectly harmless, I promise you."

"Really?" She couldn't take her eyes off it as the emperor led her further into the room, twisting to keep it in sight. Sure enough, it didn't move or track her like the other one had and there were no red lights in its "eyes." "The others in the corridors have a pilot who keeps them on standby apparently."

She hadn't figured out exactly how that worked yet, nor had she seen any warrior who she thought might be one of the bot pilots. She assumed the Lathar had a similar structure to Terran forces, with ground troops like Sardaan and his men with separate groups for air and space combat pilots.

"Absolutely. It's on a different protocol to the ship bots, solely centered around personal protection. It won't activate unless there is a personal threat to me. Please, take a seat." Daaynal indicated one of the huge couches set around a small, low table. On Earth she'd have called it a coffee table, but she had no idea what the Latharian equivalent was.

"I guess I shouldn't attack you with the fruit bowl then," she said with a smile, as she perched on the edge of one of the couches. They were massive, obviously designed to hold men as large as Daaynal himself. If she sat back, she'd disappear into the cushions. Not a very dignified position when dealing with an emperor.

Not when she wanted something from him.

"No, indeed," he chuckled. "That would probably not be the wisest move."

She tilted her head as he took a seat opposite her, elbows resting lightly on his knees and his strong fingers laced together. Although his rooms seemed to be filled with priceless antiques and expensive furnishings, the man himself was dressed like any other Latharian warrior she'd seen. And the fact he had more braids in his hair than Sardaan hadn't escaped her notice.

"What?" he asked, obviously picking up on her interest. His lips quirked up into a small smile. "Do I have something on my nose?"

She couldn't help but smile. Daaynal had a relaxed manner that put people at ease quickly—if you discounted the studied nonchalance in his big frame and ignored the tension and power coiled beneath.

"No. I'm curious," she admitted, sweeping a hand around them. "You have all this and still you dress like just a warrior..."

His smile deepened. "I am a warrior. Like all the rest, I have to watch my back to maintain my position." He leaned against the low back of the couch, arms spread wide. The movement had his jacket opening down the center, revealing a body that was honed and carved by physical training. "Perhaps more so... every male wants to be emperor. Few understand it's not about the power. It's about sacrifice as well."

The lonely note in his voice struck her and she looked at him. *Really* looked at him. There was a hardness there, and also a bitterness.

"Would you walk away from it all?" she asked suddenly. "If you had the chance to?"

"*Draanth* yes," he replied instantly and then chuckled, looking away from her for a moment and lifting a hand to rub over his stubbled jaw. When he looked back at her, his green eyes were alight with amusement. "Are you sure you're just a soldier, Major General? Because you'd make a damn good interrogator."

She chuckled. "Just a grunt, sorry. I leave all that stuff to the professionals."

"Well... if you change your mind, I'm sure I can find a job for you on my staff."

There it was. The opening she was looking for.

"Actually," she said, leaning forward. "I did want to talk to you about a job, but not as an interrogator."

He didn't move, watching her with an unblinking gaze. "Oh?"

Dammit. He was going to make her spell it out, was he? She hid her frustration and simply met his intense gaze. If he thought that was going to overset her, he had another think coming. She was made of far sterner stuff.

"I wanted to offer you an opportunity." He didn't speak so she carried on, but not quickly. She wouldn't fall into that trap and put herself on the back foot. Instead her voice was measured and her gaze on his firm. She needed to come at this from a position of power, even though she really didn't have one. Sometimes the illusion was all that was needed. "I wanted to offer you my help in understanding human culture and negotiating with my people."

"Why would I need that?" His expression didn't alter, intent on hers. "I already have human advisors. My sister-sons' mates are both human. Both bonded to Latharian warriors and happy to—"

He stopped talking suddenly, his eyes narrowing. She had only a second's warning as the lights went out in the room, plunging them into blackness. Instantly, her instincts and training went into high alert. She hit the deck, palming the dagger from her boot, as the sound of metallic clunking filled the room, the air right above her moving as something big and heavy flew overhead.

A strange sound cut through the air, like it was being parted with something sharper than steel or light. The scuff of a boot danced with clicking like metallic spider feet. She held her breath as her heart jumped into her throat.

The bot was active in the room. It had to be. Without being able to see, there was no safe place to run. She fought down the fear. It wasn't after her. If it had seen her as a threat, she would have been dead as soon as she'd entered the room. Which meant there was someone else in here.

Another whoosh and the sensation of movement. A hard hand grabbed her upper arm and she yelped, trying to fight off her attacker, only to be pulled up against a solid body as her strike was blocked with a hard arm.

"Quiet, female," Daaynal's voice rasped in her ear. "There's more than one."

She nodded, even though he couldn't see, sliding back to back with the big Lathar. He moved easily, a reassuring presence.

A strangled scream that turned into a wet gurgle cut the silence and then Daaynal was gone. Another thud reached her ears, like a body hitting the floor, and then the doors slid open, light slicing through to illuminate a scene right out of a horror film...

SARDAAN HAD SEEN many dead warriors. The life of a Lathar was often brutal and violent. Death was an inevitable part of it. Battles were common, injuries even more so, and he'd been to pay his respects in halls like this many times before. It never got any easier.

Aariin was laid out on the altar, beneath the symbol of the mother goddess. Like all warriors he wore his leathers, his weapons at his side for his journey to the life beyond. Sardaan took a few steps forward to reach the altar.

Isan had done a good job. Apart from the fact he was pale, Sardaan could almost believe the young warrior was asleep. The horrendous wound that had almost cleaved his chest in two was covered by his combat jacket, the edge of a sealed wound just visible by his throat.

Sardaan rubbed a hand over his eyes tiredly. He'd contacted Aariin's father to let him know the fate of his son. The older warrior had merely shrugged. No, he did not want his family colors given to the boy at the rites. The boy was *Quesen*, he'd said. Third born to an oonat, thus not an heir.

Not important.

Not worthy.

Silently, Sardaan unfolded the fabric over his arm and draped it over the body of the younger man. His colors were that of a minor line of the K'Vass, but something was better than nothing. And, as the last remaining member of his family, he had the right to grant them to whomever he pleased. In life or death.

"Go into the next life with honor, brother," he murmured in a low voice, hand clenched over his heart in the traditional salute before turning and leaving the hall.

Shaking his hair back, he forced his mind to return from contemplation to the present. Back to Dani. His mate. She was finally and properly his mate. He never thought he'd be lucky enough to have one, ever. Like most Lathar of his age, he'd consigned himself to a lifetime of solitude, brightened only by the comradeship of his brothers in arms and the occasional visit to the pleasure houses.

Some warriors had resorted to taking concubines from other races. There were several in the galaxy, but most weren't genetically compatible with the Lathar. Hell, he'd even heard tell of one Lathar, a C'Vaal he believed, had taken a Krynassis female as his mate. He bit back a snort. He'd like to see how *that* played out for the C'Vaal. But then... that clan were more pirates than warriors. They had to be given their territory out in the Deniar expanse. Still, Krynassis females were rare and queens were very protective of their female offspring.

Unlike some, the idea of taking an oonat concubine had filled him with revulsion. He'd long ago decided that when he needed an heir to continue his line, he would have his seed implanted rather than bed one. He'd always held off on that, hoping the healers would perfect the ex-vitro technology they'd been working on for years.

He shook the thoughts off. He wouldn't need to worry about implantation or concubines now he had Dani. His mate. Pleasant memories of their night together filled his mind as he walked down the corridor. Heat filled him at one specific memory— the feeling of her tiny body beneath his.

She was obviously a warrior, with a slender, taut figure packed with lean muscles... but she was also soft and giving in all the right places. And the heaven of being balls deep in the silken embrace of her tight body... he shuddered with pleasure at the memory. Perhaps he could sneak back to their quarters between training and his shift on the bridge?

"Computer. Locate my mate," he ordered aloud, knowing the ship's computer system would pick up his command, a small buzz of pride filling him at the words.

He only had to wait a couple of seconds for a reply, the smooth gender-neutral voice of the ship answering him. "Danielle K'Vass is currently located in the Imperial Suite."

He paused mid-stride, a frown creasing his brow. In the Imperial Suite? Why was Dani in the Imperial Suite?

"Computer, locate His Majesty, Daaynal K'Saan," he said carefully, ignoring the strange feeling in the center of his chest. Why was his mate in the Imperial Suite?

"The emperor is in the Imperial Suite."

Fear slammed through Sardaan like a supernova. She was trying to leave him. That was the only reason he could think of that she'd be in the emperor's rooms. To petition Daaynal to release her from his claim and let her go home.

He went from a walk to a flat-out sprint within a heartbeat. His heart pounded with fear, a cold sweat sliding down his spine. She couldn't leave him. She was *his* and no one, not even the emperor himself, would take her from him. Ever. Even if he had to challenge Daaynal himself.

"MOVE!" he bellowed as a squad turned the corner and filled the corridor ahead of him. They scattered, which was fortunate, since he'd have bowled them out of the way if need be. He ignored the yells and curses as they were left behind him.

Turning the corner, he growled as he realized there was another squad of warriors ahead of him. At his bellow, they scattered. He was halfway past them when the faces registered. It was the *Quesen* squad.

"What's going on? Is there an alert?" Riis called out, and the corridor was filled with the sound of running feet as the young warriors sprinted to catch up with him.

"Dani. The emperor's suite," he bit out, outpacing them all in his fear.

He had to get there in time. Lady, he *had* to get there in time. He wouldn't lose her when he'd only just found her. He *couldn't*. Skidding around the corner, he all but slammed into the doors to the Imperial Suite. They slid open and he nearly fell through, so desperate was he to get inside.

"Where is she?" he growled dangerously,

advancing on the aide behind the desk. The male had shot to his feet, getting between Sardaan and the door to the emperor's rooms. They didn't slide open automatically, obviously DNA locked. Only the emperor and his trusted staff would be able to open them. Sardaan's eyes narrowed.

And the emperor had his mate in there.

"No! You can't go in there!" the aide insisted, only to find the bigger warrior's hand about his throat as Sardaan slammed him into the wall by the door.

"Open it," he ordered, his hand cutting the other male's air off. "My mate is in there. Open it *now.*"

The added encouragement of his dagger pressed up under the male's jaw and the appearance of the *Quesen* team behind him seemed to just the incentive the warrior needed and, with a small gasp, he reached out and slapped his palm over the entry-plate on the door.

The door slid open, illuminating the room within. It was painted scarlet with blood. For a moment, he stared at the scene of chaos. The room was filled with grim-faced warriors attacking two people in the center of the room. The emperor bellowed with rage as he fought back, a ... Sardaan's heart all but stopped... a slender female figure fighting back to back with him as the big *drakeen* bot skittered and danced around him, keeping the thick of the attackers away and stopping the pair from being overwhelmed.

"*QUESEN ASENDAR!*" Sardaan bellowed, ordering the warriors behind him into battle. They reacted instantly, flooding the room and hitting the emperor's attackers from the rear with all the speed and ferocity of the highest trained warriors. Pinned in between their target and the new group at the rear, the attacking group was soon cut down. Sardaan himself accounted for many of them, cutting them down with the heavy combat daggers sheathed in his boots.

Then there was just one. His gaze narrowed as he recognized Ter T'Raniis, half his face covered in blood and a snarl of fury on his face as he stood in the middle of his fallen warriors. Sardaan's lip curled back. First Aariin and now a failed assassination attempt on the emperor himself? Ter was either delusional or suicidal.

"He's mine," Sardaan snarled as the emperor's *drakeen* bodyguard skittered forward. It stopped instantly at his words, without a signal from Daaynal himself. Further proof to the rumor that the Imperial bots were piloted by the man himself.

"Come on then, T'Raniis..." Sardaan's voice was low and dangerous. "Let's see what you've got."

Ter laughed, the sound malicious as he focused on Sardaan. He had to know he wasn't getting out of this alive. "Come on then. I'll split you in two like that little *Quesen* you got so bent out of shape over. Then I'll claim your woman for myself."

Mentioning Aariin was the wrong move. Threatening Dani was an even worse one. White hot fury exploded through Sardaan's veins like an *antorian* dump into an engine's fuel injectors. He went from standing into motion within a heartbeat, his blades slicing through the air like glittering arcs of moving death. He didn't bother with any posturing. No special moves. Nothing fancy. Instead he used brute force and speed to take both blades through Ter's neck. Side to side. The lethally sharp blades sliced through skin, flesh, arteries and vertebrae as if they weren't even there.

Ter blinked as Sardaan finished the movement, his arms spread out to the side, blades dripping blood. For anyone watching who hadn't seen the whole thing, he would have looked wide open, his face, throat and torso vulnerable to any attack Ter might launch.

But the other warrior wasn't going to attack. Even

though he blinked slowly, the movement was simply the reaction of his dying brain as, slowly, his head slid to one side while his body slid the other way. His corpse hit the floor in two dull thuds, already ignored by Sardaan as he whirled around. He'd avenged Aariin. Now it was time to find his mate.

His gaze immediately latched on to the slender figure in the middle of the carnage, blade in her hand. Relief hit him in a cold rush and he crossed the distance to haul her into his arms before he'd taken his next breath.

"Traitor!" Daaynal bellowed, striding forward at the same moment the aide in the doorway made a run for it. The aide pulled up sharply as the *Quesen* blocked his escape. A flick of his wrists later and he had a blade in each hand. The young warriors didn't flinch, watching him with hard expressions. Pride filled Sardaan when the older warrior roared and tried to rush them, expecting them to scatter as they usually did.

Instead, they stood their ground. More than. With an answering bellow, they met his attack, using a combination of the moves Sardaan had been drilling into them and the ones they'd learned from Kenna and Dani. The clash of blades and grunts filled the room as they surrounded the aide. He was forced to defend himself on all sides, his expression changing from grim determination to concern, and finally to fear as the realization he couldn't beat the *Quesen* flitted across his face.

Riis moved in when he tried a sleight of hand stab to the ribcage of a warrior who'd left an opening. He grunted and twisted to avoid it and then yanked the guy toward him, spinning him around into a deadly embrace. A hard arm over the front of the guy's throat, he cut his air off.

"Don't kill him," Daaynal ordered as Riis' shoulders bunched, ready for a neck-breaker move. The barked order stopped him in his tracks and he simply tightened his hold until the male stopped thrashing. Letting go of the limp form, he allowed the male to fall to the floor.

The threat dealt with, Sardaan concentrated on Dani. He was torn between holding her and checking her over. There was a splash of blood across her thigh. His gaze narrowed as he yanked her closer, checking her leg.

"Sardaan, I'm fine!" She smiled, grabbing for his hands. "I promise. I'm okay."

"Thank the gods," he breathed, pulling her closer. "You about killed me there, female. I thought you'd been killed. Worse..."

She chuckled, smoothing her hands over his shoulders. The touch helped ease the tension running through his body. Holding her against him, feeling her tiny form tucked against his, helped. "What could be worse than me being killed? You guys don't have zombies or anything, right?"

"Zombies?" He shook his head. "I have no idea what that is."

He wrapped his arms around her, his lips against her hair on the top of her head. Inhaling, he dragged her scent deep into his lungs.

"I thought you were trying to leave me," he admitted raggedly. "I thought you'd come to ask the emperor to release you from our mating."

She pulled back, surprise in her eyes. "No... why would I do that? I came here to ask him for a job."

"Indeed," Daaynal stepped forward, the big *drakeen* bot sidling backward to its charging alcove. The metallic glint of a pilot's uplink band was just visible in the fall of his dark hair. He completely ignored the dead males on the floor, focusing on the couple. "And I have decided to accept. Your mate has become our new human-Latharian liaison officer."

13

*H*e wanted her to stay.

So much so that as soon as the emperor gave them permission to leave so he could deal with the aide who'd been part of the assassination plot against him, Sardaan had whisked Dani right back to his quarters. He'd spend the next couple of hours proving exactly how much... desperately taking her as though he expected her to be snatched away at any moment. She shivered as she lay in the middle of the rumpled sheets, tired and replete, watching her handsome mate dress for the second time that day.

She rolled to her knees and crawled forward, wrapping her arms around his neck. "Do you have to go on bridge duty *right* now?"

He shifted position, dropping his shoulder and pulling her into his lap for a long, hard kiss. She melted against him, her arms still around his neck. The heat of his body against hers made her shiver again, even though they'd just finished. By the time he broke the kiss, both their breathing was compromised.

"You are *far* too much of a temptation, little mate," he rumbled in a deep voice. "But yes, I do. I don't want to earn Danaar's ire. He's already pissed that the vice president went back to your ship. I don't need to make that worse by neglecting my duty."

Dani slid out of his lap as he put his boots on. "Danaar and Madison Cole?"

She'd only spoken to the ship's acting commander once before, but the impression of a tall, growly, intensely focused man had stuck in her mind. He wasn't at all the sort she'd find either approachable or attractive. The idea of him and Madison Cole...

"He likes her then?"

Sardaan nodded. "Like she's the moon to his sun. I'm surprised he didn't try and claim her while she was aboard."

Dani snorted in amusement. "Have you *met* Madison Cole? Shit, the woman scares even me. I'd rather take the All-Trial against your damn combat bots than face her in a bad mood."

He grinned as he looked over his shoulder. The lights by the side of the bed caught his unusual eyes, making her shiver. He really was the most beautiful man she'd ever seen. Of course, it helped that she was halfway in love with him.

Existence paused in the second between one heartbeat and the next.

Halfway in love with him... No, she wasn't *halfway* in love with him. She was completely and utterly head over heels in love with her sexy alien husband.

Her eyes fluttered closed for a second. How... when had that happened? She'd been so determined, knowing the danger he posed to her heart, to not allow it to happen. But somehow, he'd gotten past all her defenses anyway, found a place for himself in her heart. And...

She didn't want to let him go. Ever.

Surging forward, she wrapped her arms around him suddenly from behind and kissed the side of his neck.

The deep chuckle he gave vibrated through his back where she pressed against him, his hand over her wrists where they crossed on his chest. "What was that for? Not that I'm complaining..."

"Nothing." She pressed her face into the curve where his neck met his shoulder for a moment and then lifted up. She nipped lightly at his ear and smiled as he sucked a hard breath in. "Why? Don't you like it?"

The chuckle was replaced by a deep, warning growl. "Oh, I like it. Carry on like that though, and I'll have you flat on your back, my cock buried balls deep in your tight little pussy before you can say the word."

Heat slammed into her without warning and he chuckled at her needy little gasp, turning to plant a hard kiss on her lips. "Hold that thought... for later."

She was still reeling from the kiss as he stood, grabbing his jacket from the hook by the door. Then, with a wink and a heat-filled glance, he left for the bridge.

Flopping back on the bed, she grabbed the pillow and held it to herself. It smelled of him, so she buried her face in it and breathed in deeply. Adjusting to her new normal would take a while but... she smiled to herself. She would do it.

Somehow. With her new job as liaison officer, and him, they could make anything work.

A soft chirping got her attention and she lifted her head. What was that? She frowned as she looked around, finally spotting the blinking light on the console over the desk. It hadn't been there before. She was sure of it. And the sound definitely hadn't.

Sliding from the bed, she wrapped one of Sardaan's shirts around her like a bathrobe. It might as well have been, the warm, silky fabric hitting her at mid-thigh and, more importantly, covering her completely. Reaching the desk, she stood in front of it for a moment. The console was unfamiliar to her and the keys she could see were all in Latharian.

"Hello?"

She leaned forward to wave her hand in front of the little blinking light. It didn't look like a power light. A screen burst into life out of nowhere. Even though she'd been briefed on Latharian tech, it still made her jump. Thankfully, she managed not to squeak or anything equally embarrassing. It had been bad enough to realize that she had been utterly useless in the fight in the emperor's quarters without making a fool of herself as well.

A face came into focus, hovering half a foot above the dark wood. It was a Latharian warrior, younger if she didn't miss her guess, with only two or three braids worked through his dark hair.

"Major General Black?" he asked, his gaze sliding past her.

"Yes. How can I help you?"

She kept her face neutral and impassive, refusing to be embarrassed by the rumpled bed behind her. Why should she? According to Latharian customs, she and Sardaan were newly married. What they got up to in the privacy of their own quarters was their own business. However, it did amuse her a little that the alien ship appeared to run on scuttlebutt and gossip just like human ones did.

The young warrior looked back at her, his gaze flicking down to her all-concealing shirt. For a moment disappointment flashed in the backs of his turquoise eyes.

"I have a communication for you. From the human vessel," he added.

She resisted the urge to lift an eyebrow. With at least five human vessels in the immediate vicinity, it could be any of them. "Of course, please put it through."

He nodded. "Patching now."

The warrior disappeared in a fuzz of visual static.

A second later the static disappeared, and a human man appeared in its place.

"Admiral Radcliffe." Her nod was perfunctory and courteous to conceal the distaste rising in the back of her throat.

Of all the people Terran Command could have fielded to engage the Lathar, and they had to throw Radcliffe into the mix. Like Hopkins, he was vehemently xenophobic and anti-Lathar, and had been banging the drum about ramping up defenses and taking on the Lathar since the moment humanity had found out about their existence.

"Black." Grizzled with gray hair and a gruff voice, the Admiral merely nodded curtly, his gaze cutting to someone off screen. His image wavered for a moment and then he asked, "Are we secure now?"

"*Yes, Admiral. Level five encryption protocols running. But I don't know how long I can keep the line secure.*"

"Don't tell me what you can't do, young man," Radcliffe snarled. "Make it happen or I'll have you in the brig." His attention focused back onto Dani.

"Black. Report. What have you found out about these blasted aliens?"

She kept her irritation under wraps by a supreme effort of will.

"They're highly intelligent—"

"Nonsense!" The admiral broke in, cutting her off. "They're bloody barbarians who still fight with swords!"

"They are a warrior culture," she continued, her voice firm, as though he hadn't said a word. "The bladed weapons appear to be mainly used in one-on-one honor bouts and as personal weaponry for higher ranked individuals. Their combat units are well trained and well-armed. I've seen evidence of what looks like assault rifles and they're not what we need to be careful of."

"Oh?" The admiral leaned forward, interest in his dark eyes. His mustache was impressive, blunt-cut over his mouth. For some reason the fact that it was obviously well-kept and groomed pissed her off just as much as the bling and braid the guy wore. Why couldn't they have sent General McGowan? Same rank, but different branch and with shit-loads more experience in unusual battle situations.

"The combat bots." Her voice was flat, verging on incredulous. Seriously? Had this guy not been briefed at all... not seen the footage from the Sentinel? "Like the ones they used on the Sentinel. They're fast, agile and very difficult to put down."

He chuckled, amusement obvious. "I'm sure our marines can handle a few dumb robots."

She just looked at him. "That's my point, *sir*. They aren't dumb robots. They're piloted by experienced Latharian warriors. And I might point out, Sentinel five had several units of battle-hardened marines. It made fuck all difference."

Anger flashed in Radcliffe's eyes. Used to it, she ignored the look. Same old, same old. He was an Old Boys Club, dyed in the wool soldier who didn't like being corrected by a woman. Even when she was fucking right.

"Yeah, but they don't have the advantage we do."

Advantage? She leaned forward a little. "Oh?"

Radcliffe grinned at her. It wasn't a nice expression. "You, Major General. You're going to find us some weaknesses in their defense that we can punch through."

She couldn't help it, the snort of laughter burst from her before she could stop it. "Weaknesses? Not likely. From what I can tell, they've been at war with pretty much everyone for hundreds of years. They're fucking good at it."

She leveled a hard look at him. "Plus. I am not a spy. What happened to negotiations with the Lathar?"

Even an idiot could see that there was no way humanity could wage a war against the Lathar. Not and win anyway. However, they *could* wage a war and find themselves completely and utterly defeated.

Not wiped out. No. She'd read between the lines enough to know what would happen.

"Admiral, do not pick this fight," she warned. "We cannot win against this enemy. If we try, they will annihilate us. Utterly. They'll destroy our forces and then raze Earth and all her colonies. You've got a daughter, right? Well, she and every other fertile female will be enslaved and given to alien men to bear their children. Humanity will disappear within a generation. Do you want that?"

He shook his head. "Not going to happen, Major General, because *you* are going to find a way for us to get on that ship and kidnap this emperor of theirs. Once we have him, they will capitulate."

He was insane.

Dani was forced to sit there for a moment as his words registered. They were going to try and kidnap the Latharian emperor... the man she'd seen just hours ago shrug off an assassination attempt.

"Or..." Radcliffe was still speaking. "Your second in command... remember her before you decided to fuck an alien? Yeah, she's going to be facing charges.

Conduct unbecoming with an officer under her command."

Shit. He really was hitting below the belt. Her face set.

"I'll get you on the ship," she said, her voice cold and hard. "But the rest is totally on your head. I don't know enough about Latharian troop movements or strength to anticipate what resistance you'll face. And," she added, knowing that the call was being recorded on Radcliffe's side. "I want it on record that I think this is a bad idea."

Radcliffe just looked at her and she knew in that instant she'd made an enemy. Given half a chance, Radcliffe would have her up in front of a court martial and end her career in a heartbeat.

"Black, you lost the right to say anything in this the moment you started sleeping with the enemy." His gaze flicked to the bed behind her and detoured back to her eyes by way of the shirt wrapped around her. That it wasn't human was obvious.

He leaned forward.

"You have ten hours to get us a way onto that ship, or your friend's neck is on the line. I hear Mirax Ruas is lovely this time of year." He cut the comms leaving Dani looking at the blank wall behind the desk.

"Fucking *asshole!*" she hissed, slamming her hands flat against the hard wood of the desk. Mirax Ruas was a high security facility, one with a brutal reputation. Life expectancy there was measured in months, not years.

Which meant, unless she did something... betrayed her new husband and his people... she would be handing her friend a death sentence.

14

*S*he could do this. All she had to do was crack an alien computer system, in a language she didn't understand, and drop the defense systems of a technologically advanced warship. In... she checked the timestamp on the console in front of her... under ten minutes.

Cold sweat slithered down her spine. It had taken her hours to get anywhere near a critical system she could use. Using her new role as Latharian-Terran liaison, she'd managed to get Sardaan to give her a tour of the ship.

It hadn't been a long tour but it had taken them far longer than necessary given the different nooks and crannies her alien husband had found to pull her into and kiss her senseless. The third time it had been too much for her, her need too much for her to ignore, and he'd taken her hard and fast up against the wall in here.

What he hadn't realized was she'd noted exactly what the room was, namely one of the ship's core control rooms and—she fished for something hidden in her waistband—that she'd stolen his identity tag at the same time.

One excuse about being worn out and needing a nap later and she'd slowly made her way back here. On their tour she'd worked out which areas held the combat bots and easily avoided them. Once she'd figured out the logic of the Latharian ship, working her way through it without being detected had been easy.

Figuring out the computer system once she was in, though, was a completely different matter.

"Come on, Dani," she muttered to herself as she studied the screen. "How difficult can this be?"

Finally, after much scrolling about, she took a chance. The Lathar might be an alien race, but by all accounts, they were related to humanity. She wasn't going so far as to believe they were the ancestors of the human race. At most, like the usual absentee parent, they'd merely donated some DNA. The rest mankind had done on their own.

But, that being said, they were a bipedal species. Two arms. Two legs. Almost identical brain. Which meant she should be able to find something. Some similarity she could use to work this out.

Plus... the Latharian language *looked* familiar. Almost as if she squinted her eyes and looked at it right, it would start to make sense.

Poking at one of the symbols, she was rewarded with another screen, one full of more Latharian glyphs. On a hunch, she pressed another and hissed in triumph as a schematic of the ship filled the screen. As she watched, the language on the screen shifted, morphing into English.

Her eyes widened.

It wasn't just a diagram of all the decks, but different colors denoted the shielding and... She leaned forward, frowning.

"Shit," she breathed.

It even had the combat bot alcoves on here.

"No way. It can't be this easy, surely?" she murmured, her hand hovering over the map.

Sudden guilt hit her, her stomach clenching in on itself hard. The import of what she was about to do hit her. If she did this, people would die. Both human and Lathar. Men and women she'd served with, commanded... Lathar she'd met here. Isan,

Danaar, Riis... Sardaan. She closed her eyes, dread filling her soul. Even her new husband would be in danger. Might even be killed.

Her breath escaped her lungs in a shuddering sigh. Sardaan was a soldier, though. Like her, he knew the risks of what they did and accepted them. And, with the technology of the Lathar, he had more than a fighting chance.

Shannon didn't have a chance though. If Dani didn't do this, Shannon was on a one-way trip to Mirax Ruas. And that was a death sentence. She couldn't do that to Shannon, not if she could stop it.

Opening her eyes, she pressed buttons on the screen quickly, setting the shields and bots to shut down at precisely the same time as the human attack. Her heart pounded like she'd run a marathon as she pressed the button to confirm the order.

Shutting the screen down quickly, she turned to escape the room. She'd done what was ordered and given Radcliffe's force the opening they needed to get onto the ship. That was all she was going to do.

The doors slid open in front of her and she stopped dead. There, framed in the doorway, were two heavy combat bots, their red eyes fixed balefully on her.

She held her ground, hands out to the side in

surrender and cold sweat slithering down her spine as they advanced on her. Their metallic feet clicked heavily against the deck plating.

"I need to speak to Sardaan K'Vass," she announced, looking at the one on her left. They moved too easily, too much like spiders. The stuff of nightmares.

She held eye contact with the red eye, knowing that the pilot would be able to hear her. "Please. I have information for him. On an imminent human attack."

They moved without warning and she was forced to stifle a startled cry as metal "hands" closed around her wrists like manacles. Her heart pounded against her chest, her breathing shortening as they dragged her from the room.

SHE'D BETRAYED HIM.

Sardaan gripped the edge of his console so tightly, he'd probably leave marks in the indestructible metal. His beautiful human mate, who he'd thought was settling in and getting used to their way of life, had betrayed him.

His mate was a faithless, lying little human bitch.

He closed his eyes for a second as he stood at his console, his body taking over and trying to block out the sight of her on the screen, taking down all their defenses. He'd watched the scene play out in utter disbelief, unable to believe she could betray him.

Not after the passion they'd shared... not after how sweetly she'd submitted to him and moaned for him in his bed. But she had, and with that betrayal the final pieces of the puzzle that the humans posed had fallen into place.

They'd been aware of the humans marshalling an attack for the past couple of hours. Oh, they'd thought they were being clever, hiding their attack ships on the other side of the ship nearest to the *Veral'vias*. In the shadows where they thought the Lathar couldn't see them.

It was almost as if they didn't realize the Latharian scanners could pick up the energy signatures of their engines. Of the powered-up weaponry on board. Cutting lasers, no matter what race had built them, were distinctive. As soon as the *Veral'vias* had registered them on scans, alarm bells had started to ring.

At first, there had been laughter on the bridge. After all, what could the humans possibly hope to achieve with their tiny little assault ships against the might of the *Veral'vias?* Not only did it massively outpower the human ships, but they'd need planet killer level tech to even scratch its shielding.

Convinced that the ships sheltered behind the human battleship like children hiding behind their mother's skirts was a distraction, Sardaan had run detailed scans looking for the real attack.

He hadn't found anything.

It had taken him a moment to realize there *wasn't* a more complicated attack. That the small group of ships *was* the Terran plan.

The entire bridge had fallen silent at that point, Danaar, Fenriis' second in command and acting commander speaking for them all when he'd said, "Seriously? Did they miss the fact we could blow their entire fleet out of space?"

No one answered that question. No one could. It seemed that yes, the humans *had* either missed that point entirely or didn't care and planned on attacking anyway. Perhaps they planned on throwing themselves at the Latharian shields, dashing themselves to pieces in some sort of ultimate defiance...

"Unauthorized access to the computer systems."

"What the hell are they playing at?" Danaar

growled from the center of the bridge. "Find me that unauthorized access!"

"On it," Sardaan replied. His hands flew over the console in front of him as he tracked the recent commands through the system. At first he'd assumed the humans had somehow managed to hack through the AI's firewalls but there was no intrusion. There couldn't be, not with their primitive systems.

Then he found it. The source of the commands was in a secondary control room up on the seventh level. His eyes closed as he recognized the location instantly. The room he'd taken Dani in, hard and fast up against the wall during their tour of the ship earlier. From there it had been a quick task to filter through the internal sensors and bring the feed up for the room. Roll the timeframe back...

"I found the unauthorized access," he said, his voice locked down and emotionless. "Putting on the main screen now."

He didn't look as Dani appeared on the main screen, seeing it all on the console in front of him. He hardened his heart at the sight of her sitting in front of the console, trying to figure out their language, so different from her own. A little sense of pride wanted to roll through him when she worked it out quickly, but he stamped it down.

His expression didn't soften even when she seemed to debate her decision, a look of what appeared to be pain crossing her beautiful features. She took the shields and bots offline in quick, decisive movements.

"Avatars dispatched to ingress location," he added. "They'll take her into custody and bring her here."

Danaar looked over at him, his expression level. "She's your mate. You will be responsible for carrying out the appropriate discipline."

Sardaan nodded. "I will deal with her. What sanctions have you decided upon, Commander?"

He waited by his console, his entire frame tight. Dani had put them all at risk, could have cost thousands of warriors' lives. But... even as mad at her as he was... he didn't think he could kill her, not even if Danaar ordered him to.

"The intrusion was discovered quickly," the big Latharian rumbled in a low voice. "Shields are back online and no harm was done. Discipline your female, warrior, in whatever way you see fit. Find out why and what else the humans have planned... I don't care how you get that information, but get it. Meanwhile, we'll allow the humans to continue, thinking their plan has worked, and see what they do next."

"Yes, War Commander." He stood up straight, hand over his heart in the traditional salute. "Permission to leave the bridge?"

"Granted."

Sardaan turned back to his duty station for a moment, sending a signal to the avatar pilots to take his faithless mate directly to the cells. Signing off and handing over to the warrior who stepped up to replace him, he left the bridge quickly.

"No, please. I need to speak to Sardaan K'Vass," Dani protested as the metal monsters hauled her into a cell in the lower levels of the ship. She'd tried to fight, dig her heels in, but she was no match for their non-human strength. They'd simply hauled her off her feet, and it became a case of walk or be dragged. She had enough dignity to want to walk.

But the sight of the cell door looming largely ahead of her like the cavernous maw of some space beast, ready to swallow her up whole, changed all that. Fear lanced her, the sure feeling that if she let herself be taken in there she would never get out.

"No! *No!*" She struggled against the metal monsters so violently one of them lurched to the side. Hope filled her. Perhaps she *could* fight them. She redoubled her efforts, throwing her weight from side to side in an effort to knock them off balance. If she could just get one wrist free...

They moved in concert, yanking her arms up above her head until her toes only just grazed the floor. A soft cry escaped her lips, fire racing down her arms from her wrists to her shoulders as she was suspended.

She closed her eyes, her head dropping forward in defeat. She couldn't fight them after all. They were just too powerful. Her heart thundered in her chest, her breathing shortened as they dragged her through the doorway into the cell. It was dark and dank, something dripping down the wall in the far corner.

The monsters pulled her to the center of the room and the clamp of their metal hands was replaced with the hard band of manacles as they chained her up. The chains above her head rattled slightly with her weight as they let her go. She was on her tiptoes still, her entire body taut.

The machines turned and stomped out of the cell, the door clanging shut with a resounding crash behind them. Silence filled the room, only relieved by the drip-drip-drip in the corner and the soft rasp of her breath.

Waiting a few minutes longer to be sure that the machines were actually gone, she lifted her head. She might have lost the battle, but she wasn't down and out. The "war" was still to be won. She looked up at her bonds. There were heavy manacles around her wrists attached to chains. She squinted up into the darkness above. The light didn't reach that far up, but it looked like the chain her manacles were attached to was simply looped over a hook up there.

If she could get up there somehow, she could unhook herself. She'd still be in the cell, but she wouldn't be as helpless as she was now.

Her lips compressed with grim determination. Lifting up as high as she could, she got a grip on the chains above her manacles. A sharp tug on them proved they were solid.

Gathering herself, she tensed her body and pulled upward. Smoothly, she folded herself up, pushing upward with her legs. Her feet just brushed something overhead but didn't catch it properly. She hissed, the muscles in her shoulders burning, but she held on. Tensing her stomach muscles, she pushed further, her body screaming from the exertion as lactic acid began to build.

Finally, she managed to get a foot over whatever it was up there. She hoped it was a pipe. Thoughts of more of the metal combat machines hidden up there in the darkness sent a cold sweat slithering down her spine. At any moment she expected those dagger-like claws to punch through her thigh as she hooked first one leg and then the other over the pipe.

It was still dark up there. She hung like a bat for a few moments, waiting for her eyes to adjust. After a few moments they did, and the inky darkness yielded to a world of gray and black.

She'd been right. The chain attached to her manacles was simply looped over a hook on the pipe. Her gaze traveled along it, noting three more. The cell could hold four. She was thankful she was the only one. Because if she could lift herself up here and get free, then damn sure a Latharian warrior could.

Still hanging upside down, she started to lift the chain off the hook and grunted as it wouldn't move. She wriggled closer to look, feeling along the links to see what the problem was. It didn't take her long.

Obviously the chains were used to hold prisoners a lot heavier than she was. Over time, and presumably after many pissed off prisoners thrashing about trying to break out, the metal had kinked together. It almost seemed pressure-welded in place.

Gritting her teeth, she worked at the obstruction, trying to get it loose. It fought her, refusing to budge, and she hissed as her fingers skittered across it, the sharp edge of the metal catching and ripping into her skin.

"Bastard thing!" She stuck her hurt finger in her mouth for a few seconds until it stopped smarting. Pulling it free, she shook it for a few seconds and then went right back to trying to free the chain.

After a couple of tries, both hands either side and yanking it back and forth, it gave. She fist-pumped the air in triumph, gripped the bar and unfurling her legs to drop lightly down to the metal floor.

And there she stood. Okay. She was free from the hook, but she was still in the cell. Her gaze zeroed in on the cell door, but before she could make a move toward it to try and pick the lock, the sound of booted feet echoed down the corridor.

All her senses on alert, she drew back into the

darkness, wrapping the chain around her hands. All she needed was one of the Lathar to step in here with her, and she had him. She'd choke him out and leave him hidden in the shadows, making her escape. Now that she knew the layout of the ship, it wouldn't take her long to get back to Sardaan's quarters and make him listen to her. Tell him about the attack.

15

*S*ardaan had no idea what to expect when he reached the cell they'd taken his faithless mate to, but it wasn't for the damn thing to be empty.

But it was.

The chains in the middle of the room where the prisoners were normally strung up dangled motionlessly, holding no one. Oddly, one set was missing. He dismissed it as maintenance. There was no way even an experienced Terran soldier like Dani could have escaped both the avatar bots and her chains.

"*Draanthic* idiots," he hissed as he approached the bars. A quick glance at the cell identifier on the back wall told him he was in the right block. Had the pilots gotten it wrong and taken her somewhere else? Perhaps to one of the lower blocks?

"Sardaan?"

He was about to turn away when Dani's voice sounded from the darkness at the back of the cell. He froze as she emerged slowly, hope written across her expressive face. The first time he'd seen her she'd been so self-contained he'd wondered if he would ever be able to break through her shields to the woman within. Since they'd been mated though —since he'd made her his—he'd been able to read her expressions perfectly. Not that she telegraphed them, but he'd learned to note the little changes in her body language, the light in her eyes. Nothing about her was hidden from him.

Or so he'd thought.

If you'd asked him this morning, he'd have said the strong, sexy woman he'd mated hid a soft soul and gentle core. That she was a woman who cared about those around her, cared about the few she let into her life. Now, though, after seeing her disable the ship's systems and cold-heartedly condemn them all to whatever fate the human attackers had in store for them, he wasn't so sure he knew her at all.

If he'd *ever* known her.

"Oh god, I thought they'd never tell you I was down here."

His mood darkened as he opened the cell only for her to throw herself into his arms, one arm up around his neck, the other against his chest, even though the movement was constrained by her chains. He didn't wrap his arms around her, even though he wanted to, despite what she'd done.

And that angered him all the more.

"They didn't need to tell me," he ground out between gritted teeth. He didn't know this woman. "I was the one who ordered you brought down here."

He felt the jerk of surprise and the sudden stiffness in her frame as she pulled back to look at him. The look of surprise on her face morphed into one of quickly concealed hurt. She withdrew her arms carefully, and for a second he hated the wariness that flitted across her face and rewrote the lines of her body... and then he remembered she was an accomplished actress. She'd have to be to fool him so completely he almost believed she, a human soldier, could fall for a Lathar.

"You did?"

He watched as she rebuilt herself from the sudden blow he'd dealt her. Not physical—as much as he loathed her, he couldn't raise a hand to a female—but the emotional one. No, not rebuilt herself, he reminded himself, even though it looked a lot like it. No, instead, she was stripping the layers *away* rather than adding them, reverting to the stone-cold soldier she was deep inside.

"Of course you did." Her lips quirked into a bitter smile that tugged at the heartstrings he swore he didn't have. "You knew what I'd done as soon as I did it. Didn't you? That's why those machines got to me so quickly."

She made to step back from him, but he shot out a hand, gripping the back of her neck in a hard hand. Not the gentle caress he'd used before, but tight and controlled. Keeping her in place. Ruthlessly.

Her lips compressed but he caught the flare of stubbornness in her eyes. She wouldn't cry out, no matter how much he hurt her.

"Got it in one, sweetheart." He threw the human endearment at her with a curl of his lip. He'd never again call her *kelarris*. His beloved. She didn't deserve it. Perhaps never had. "Now, you're going to tell me *everything* about the Terran plans. Leave anything out and things will go much worse for you. Understand me?"

She didn't struggle against his hold. "Before we start. What happens to me after this?"

"You don't get to ask the questions. I do," he snarled, not wanting to even think about that question, let alone its answer. His grip tightened, until her lips parted on a soft gasp. "Do. You. Understand?"

He saw the shutters come down in her eyes, but she nodded. "I understand."

Shoving her from him, he grabbed the chain that linked her hands and effortlessly hauled her hands above her head, throwing it over the hook nearest him. A quick yank on the chains activated the dampeners, deadening the nervous impulses in her arms and shoulders. The hook she'd been on must have been malfunctioning, or she'd never have been able to haul herself up and free herself.

"I don't think you do." He reached out to grip her neck again. Her mask cracked, and she flinched as he yanked her toward him.

His voice was low and dangerous as he spoke, "Now, I want to know about the human plans. Everything, or I'll make sure you regret it."

HE'D THOUGHT he'd have to pressure her, use force or violence, but Sardaan walked away from the cell less than ten minutes later with the most disturbing and hilarious news he'd ever heard.

The Terrans planned to kidnap the emperor. He couldn't work out if he wanted to laugh or be impressed by their sheer audacity if they seriously thought they could just waltz onto any Latharian ship and kidnap anyone, much less Daaynal. Not only were there hordes of Latharian warriors ready to lay down their lives protecting their emperor, but the emperor himself was possibly the scariest warrior Sardaan had ever met... possibly in recorded Latharian history. The rumors said he could pilot a whole battle group of *drakeen* while leading the charge himself.

The idea of the humans even managing to reach him... was amusing.

Even more amusing was the fact the emperor wasn't even aboard. He'd returned to his own ship with his retinue.

Sardaan's smile faded, though, as the image of Dani in chains filled his mind. She hadn't looked at him as she'd given up her people's plans, her voice level and unemotional. She'd given him *everything* but she'd refused to look at him, not even when he'd yanked her chin up. Instead, she'd just closed her eyes.

He'd put it down to her being done with him now her cover had been blown, but a little niggle of doubt in the back of his mind just wouldn't leave him. When he'd left the cell, he'd heard her sigh, the soft exhalation with a slight catch in it. When he'd looked back, her head was down, resignation in every line of her delicate frame.

His heart ached in his chest, even though he knew it was an act. It *had* to be. Otherwise... he'd just broken his mate to get what he wanted. That little flinch replayed in his mind. Over and over. He shook it off as he reached the bridge.

Danaar looked up as he walked through the door. "Did you get her to talk?"

Sardaan nodded, crossing to his duty station. "Yes. The humans plan to board and try to kidnap the emperor."

Silence fell on the bridge so complete that for a moment he thought the humans had slipped through their defenses and dropped a sonic charge. Then Danaar's shoulders started to shake, his lips splitting into a broad grin as he started to laugh. The deep, rich sound filled the bridge, as startling as the silence had been.

"I'm sorry... I thought for a moment you'd said the humans planned to kidnap the emperor?"

"I did."

Sardaan's expression didn't change. No hint of a smile on his face. As ludicrous as the idea was, a threat to the emperor was no laughing matter. It could spark a war between humanity and the Lathar.

On the one hand, that would solve a *lot* of his people's problems. A war would allow them to invade and asset strip the Terran worlds. And by that, he meant the females. Every warrior could have a mate. Several. Their reproductive problems would be over and their lines secure... And he'd never be able to look Dani in the eye again.

Not that it mattered. She was his mate, but he would release her. Send her back to Earth when all this was done. Let her people deal with her. He had no clue what they'd do with a woman... a *soldier*... who had given up all their plans, but he couldn't imagine it would be good.

Not his problem.

Danaar chuckled. "I take it they haven't realized he's no longer aboard then?"

"Nope. Doesn't appear that way. They plan to board with at least three assault teams." His hands flew over his console, and an image of the interior of the ship showed in the middle of the bridge. The warriors on the bridge all turned from their stations to look.

"AI predicts they'll breech in these locations." Three dots appeared on the outer hull. "And make their way in toward the few locations the humans know about on the ship."

Danaar growled in the back of his throat as the dots made their way to the interior of the ship, splitting off to hit different locations—the bridge, the main hall and the captain's quarters. "Your female was in the emperor's quarters. She gave him up?"

Sardaan shook his head, but then cut the motion off. He didn't want to think she had...but he didn't know her. Not like he'd thought he did.

"We have to assume she did, yes," he admitted, altering the prediction to the VIP guest quarters Daaynal had occupied while he was aboard.

Danaar nodded. "Okay. We'll give them enough rope to hang themselves then. Post extra details on the three target locations and clear the halls and corridors. Let's bring them in and pick them up when they get to their objective."

With a quiet murmur the staff went back to their

positions. The next half hour was interspersed with low voices as Danaar's orders were carried out.

"Terran ships are changing positions," a warrior from the other side of the bridge announced as the three ships in front of them fired engines briefly to settle into a new position. Normally they wouldn't have thought anything of it, dismissing the alteration in position as routine. They often did it themselves when in a battlegroup. But this time they were alert and aware.

"Ships incoming. Their cloaks are crude but holding."

"Let them come," Danaar growled.

Sardaan looked over at the big warrior sitting in the command chair. His face was set, expression brooding as he stared at the image of the human vessels on the main screen. He suspected that, given half a chance, Danaar would prefer to storm the Terran ships, both stopping the imminent sneak attack and recovering the human female he wanted.

They're not worth it, brother, he thought, going back to looking at his console as it tracked the ships sneaking toward them. Time slowed to a crawl as they waited, each breath taking an eternity. As they waited, he trawled through the recent activity logs for the ship to clear them. It was a routine task, one he might as well get done while he had some time on his hands.

He frowned as he noticed an odd reading. It was a communication coming *into* the ship, to his quarters. But no one had told him that the Terrans had contacted Dani... He tried to play the recording back, but then frowned as he found an unfamiliar encryption. It was the work of a moment to use the ship AI to break through it. As he played the recording back, his expression grew tighter. For a moment he couldn't move, every cell in his body filled with rage.

She hadn't betrayed him.

They'd threatened her. Put her in an impossible situation. Used her emotions against her.

The red alert lights illuminated the bridge, dragging him out of his rage-filled paralysis. He locked his emotions down and concentrated on his duty. There would be time for him to fetch his little mate later and beg her forgiveness. Work on making what was wrong between them right again.

"Outer hull breached," the ship's computer advised. "Internal alarms on silent."

"Bring up their progress on the main screen," Danaar ordered. With a few movements, Sardaan nodded.

"On screen."

The attention of the senior staff focused on the view screen. The three ships had breached the hull exactly where he'd predicted and after the second, the screen split to show an internal view as the Terran combat teams exited through the boarding hatches.

He had to give it to them. They were very good. They moved quickly and efficiently, in total silence. It wasn't quite how Lathar units moved, but close enough that it was recognizable. He could definitely see Dani as one of the black-clad warriors... soldiers, he corrected himself, they called their warriors soldiers instead.

His gaze latched onto the leader of the third team. That it was a woman was obvious. The slender figure was secondary to the graceful way she moved. Her face was obscured by her mask, but a strand of red hair escaped the bindings at the back of her neck. At the station next to him, Isan straightened, his gaze locked to the image on the screen like a *kinerys* hawk.

Sardaan shook his head, going back to the readings on his console. Human females were obviously sorceresses, capable of bringing any Lathar male to their knees if even Isan and Danaar had succumbed. He frowned and scratched at his wrist as the third team, the one led by the woman, deviated from the expected route.

"Find out where that team is going," Danaar bit out, obviously registering the deviation as well.

"On it," Sardaan nodded, rubbing at his wrist again. It felt like a ring of fire had encircled both his wrists. He frowned as he looked down and yanked his jacket cuff back to scratch. He must have brushed against something down in the cells.

"What the... *draanth!*"

His eyes widened as he took in the dark marks that encircled his wrists.

Mating marks.

He'd bonded to his little human mate.

His Dani.

"Third team appears to be heading for the lower levels of the ship. The *Quesen* are patrolling that area." The voice came from the other side of the bridge and struck fear into Sardaan's heart. He met Isan's gaze.

"The cells. They're after Dani."

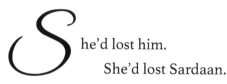She'd lost him.

She'd lost Sardaan.

The man she loved.

Dani closed her eyes and slumped in her chains, emotionally drained. No... she wasn't drained. She was numb. The place in the center of her chest where her heart normally lay was dead. Cold.

In a way she was grateful, but she knew it was little more than a small reprieve. When the numbness wore off, the ragged hole in the center of her chest where her heart had been ripped out would swamp her in agony.

She'd lost her mate—the alien husband she hadn't wanted at first but now couldn't live without. Quite when she'd fallen for him she didn't know. It didn't matter. She had fallen. Hard and fast. A bitter snort escaped her, the sound emerging as one of misery. Like a wounded animal, her voice betrayed the pain she didn't... couldn't feel at the moment.

She'd lost him. She'd known that as soon as she'd looked into his eyes and he'd looked back at her as though he didn't even know her. He'd looked right through her—cold—and in that instant her heart had broken in two.

He'd questioned her. So many questions.

She'd answered them all. Given him everything he wanted. Not because he'd threatened to hit her, or hurt her physically... she let go a shuddering breath, not wanting to know the answer to whether he would or not. She'd thought she'd known him, thought they had a real connection despite the difference in their cultures. A tear streaked hot and wet down her cheek. Obviously not.

She'd answered all his questions but not for them. Not even to save her own skin. That she didn't care about, not anymore. She'd given him everything he wanted to stop the war she knew was coming if she didn't—because that was what *would* happen if the Terran forces kidnapped Daaynal. And it was a war they wouldn't... couldn't win.

It would signal the end of the human race as they knew it.

"Hey, Boss..."

She must have fallen into a dull doze, her mind buffering her from everything that was happening. Jerking awake at the sound of her second in command, Shannon's, voice, her first thought was that she'd fallen asleep and was imagining things.

"You gonna hang about there all day or what?"

Dani twisted with a soft rattle of chains to find Shannon in the door to her cell, a combat team right behind her. The look of soft concern in the other woman's eyes almost did her in, tears hot and prickly at the backs of her eyes. She swallowed thickly and managed a smile.

"Not much in the way of in-room entertainment, so I thought I'd take a nap. What are you doing here?"

"Me 'n' the boys thought we could do with a little extra cardio," Shannon quipped as she moved into the cell, followed by a couple of the armed and masked soldiers as the others took guard positions in the corridor. Shannon reached up, a cutter in her hands.

"Look away," she ordered and cut Dani's shackles in a brief flash of violet-blue light.

Dani hissed as the pressure was relieved on her arms, pain flaring along them followed by pins and needles.

"Yeah?" She rubbed at her wrists, arching an eyebrow at the other woman. "On an alien ship?"

"Well, ya know what they say. A change is as good as a rest."

Shannon grabbed Dani's jaw and moved her face from side to side, checking her pupils. She didn't argue. Shannon had to assume she'd been worked over in the cell, and she had. Just not in the way the taller woman expected.

"You ready to be rescued?" she asked, looking into Dani's eyes. Not for blown pupils, but actually looked at her.

No. She wasn't. Even though Sardaan didn't want her, being rescued meant leaving the ship. Meant leaving him.

She nodded, blowing out a shaky breath. "Hell yes. Let's get out of here."

"Good." Shannon didn't argue, merely pressed her side-arm into Dani's hand.

Her fingers curled around it, but the reassurance the feel of the weapon in her hand would once have brought was absent. All she felt was more coldness.

More numbness. It didn't matter. Nothing mattered anymore.

"Your rescue. Lead the way."

She motioned the other woman to the front and fell in with the rest of the team as they made their way out of the cells. Moving with them, sidearm held ready, was familiar. A balm to her wounded soul. She didn't have to think. Just move. Cover her fire arcs. Watch her team's back.

No feelings. Just movement.

"Contact! Two o'clock!"

"Take cover!"

Energy blasts from Lathar weaponry split the air. The team fired back as they scattered, diving for cover along the sides of the corridor. Dani ducked behind a support strut, the thick metal shielding most of her body as she leaned out to take aim. It was hard to see for the smoke and haze in the air, but it cleared for a second and she got a look at one of the Lathar.

Riis.

Which meant the rest were *Quesen.*

"No! Stop!" she shouted as she launched herself out of cover. An energy bolt sliced through the air, grazing her arm. Agony sucked the air out of her lungs and she almost dropped the sidearm, staggering to the side.

Despite the pain, she managed to get between the team and the *Quesen*.

"STOP! They're just kids!"

The team paused, not sure what to do now she was between them and their target. The *Quesen* meanwhile, had stopped firing.

"Lady Dani," Riis called out. "Please. Step out of the way."

"I can't!" she called back over her shoulder. "They'll slaughter you where you stand."

More than that, she wasn't actually sure she *could* move. The pain in her arm was radiating through her body, overwhelming her senses. A cold sweat slithered down her spine. The only movement she was going to make would be to hit the deck plating.

"It's one section, boss... we can take them!"

"They're KIDS, for fuck's sake!"

"We are NOT kids!"

"Riis, shut the fuck up. I'm trying to save your stupid ass here!"

Sardaan and Isan exchanged glances at the

shouting echoing through the corridors from up ahead.

"Dani," Sardaan said, instantly recognizing her voice. The two warriors broke into a run. The lower levels were a rabbit warren of tunnels, maintenance ducts and worker drone shafts, so they were forced to twist and weave to reach the source of the shouting.

They reached the back of the group of *Quesen,* the youngsters parting like water as the two experienced warriors made their way to the front of the group. Dani was standing between the group of young warriors and the team of Terran soldiers, her hand out as if to stop them advancing further.

"We're—"

Dani cut Riis' argument off with a sharp movement of her hand. The other hung limply at her side. He doubted she could even lift it to aim the weapon in her hand. She'd been hit. His heart twisted at the sight of the wound across her arm, the thought of what could have happened if the bolt had hit her a couple of inches further in.

"Kids! And these are battle-hardened marines," she hissed at him, not taking her eyes off the Terrans in front of her. They all had their weapons up, aimed at the *Quesen,* but they seemed unsure, looking between Dani and the woman at the front of the team, her red hair like a banner down her back. Beside him Isan drew in a sharp breath. Sardaan ignored it with a small smile. He remembered that moment himself, when he'd first seen Dani.

"You don't stand a chance, kid, and you know it."

Her words weren't for Riis, but for the woman in front of her. The redhead wasn't looking at her any more, though. Instead, she'd registered Sardaan and Isan behind her and her weapon snapped up.

"How about us?" he asked silkily, stepping forward.

Dani gasped and whirled around. Moving quicker than he expected, she switched the weapon to her good hand, pointing it directly at him. He froze, watching her, wondering what thoughts were going through her head. Did she hate him?

Her face was smooth and emotionless as she looked at him, eyes dark. His heart sank. She'd locked herself off from him, shields to maximum. But she didn't shoot him. That was one thing at least.

Then he saw it, the slight tremble of her lower lip and the sudden tightness as she covered it up.

"Go on," he said in a soft voice, ignoring the sound of other warriors arriving and surrounding the human team. All his attention was on the woman in front of him. His mate. The woman who had called mating marks to life from within his skin.

Her hand shook, and he stepped forward, until the muzzle of the weapon pressed against the center of his chest. Over his heart. Reaching up, he plucked it out of her hand, turning her and pulling her up against his chest at the same time. She gasped but didn't struggle. She simply let him wrap her up in his arms, her head bowed.

"Deal with the rest," he ordered Isan, holding her close.

The healer nodded, his expression focused and determined as he stepped past Sardaan toward the redheaded woman.

"Holy mother of god, what the fuck happened to you?"

Sardaan turned his attention to the tiny woman in his arms. It felt good, holding her again. Feeling her smaller body nestled against him eased the terror he'd felt at the idea the Terran team had intended to rescue her. The idea that he might lose her for good, never see her again, never see her smile... hear her laugh... His arm around her tightened slightly, his knuckles white. *Draanth*, what did he say to her now?

"It's okay. It's okay," he murmured, his lips

pressed against her hair. He nodded as one of the *Quesen* stepped up with a medical wand to seal the wound on her arm. "I'm sorry, *kelarris* ... I was wrong."

At her intake of breath, he eased up on his grip and turned her gently in his arms. Her sigh was a shuddering one as he pressed her against him. She didn't relax, but the slightest bit of tension left her muscles, her frame a little less rigid as he held her. He took that as a win, his eyes closed as he breathed in her scent.

She was his. His mate. And he didn't care at all that the warriors around him could see them. Could see the way he held her close, like she was the most important thing in the world to him. Because she was. She was his entire universe, and all the stars in it.

Now he just had to convince her of that.

HE WAS SORRY.

Dani's emotions were in turmoil as they were marched up to the bridge. Hard faced warriors surrounded them as they walked, but they scared her less than Sardaan did. Or had. When he'd questioned her back in the cell, he'd looked at her like he didn't know her. Like he didn't care. Now, she didn't know. The rules had changed, and she didn't understand why.

Instead of worrying about it, she focused on the bigger picture. Radcliffe's plan had failed, just like she'd told him it would, and now they had to deal with the consequences.

"Will you just... let... me... walk!"

She turned at the sound of a furious voice to find Shannon in the healer, Isan's, arms. Barely. It wasn't a romantic embrace. Instead, his face was grim as he all but hauled her along. Finally, she managed to struggle free, making it a few steps before he grabbed her around the back of the neck and hauled her against him again.

"Asshole," she hissed into his face, but he'd used the time to get a better grip on her wrist, twisting her arm up her back. She squeaked and fought. *"Fucking asshole!"*

He moved until his hand covered the front of her throat and she stilled. "Behave," he told her firmly. "The only reason you're not in chains like the others is because of me. So. Be. Nice."

Dani closed her eyes, knowing what was coming.

Sure enough, Shannon tried to stamp on the alien healer's foot.

"Isan...stop playing with the prisoner," a new voice growled. Dani turned to find Danaar striding across the bridge toward them. His expression was grim and forbidding.

He stopped right in front of Shannon, still held still by the healer. "Talk, human. And make it fast. Don't lie either, or it will go very badly for you and your men."

"*Go to hell!*" she hissed, struggling again. Isan's hands tightened, and she gasped, her air cut off.

Dani started forward, only to be stopped by Sardaan's hard hand on her arm. He shook his head warningly. She shook it off.

"No, wait! I'm her superior officer, you talk to me." She got herself between Danaar and Shannon, glaring up at the big warrior. "I told you everything. The plan to kidnap the emperor, what kind of tactics they would use."

Shannon managed a gasp behind her, shock in her voice. "You sold us out, boss. *Why?*"

She didn't look over her shoulder, maintaining eye contact with Danaar. "Because this is a war we can't win. Radcliffe is a fucking idiot. Even if we did manage to get hold of the emperor... how long do you think we'd last before they went scorched earth policy *literally*. Humanity would become a footnote in history, remembered only because our women would become mothers for the next generation of Lathar. Our species, gone in the blink of an eye."

She lifted her chin and addressed Danaar. She knew this was on a knife's edge. She knew the emperor himself was probably listening in from somewhere. "Some of us are not idiots. The man who gave the order for this attack is. You need to speak to Vice President Cole about this."

"They can't." Shannon's voice was low. "She's gone. Out of office. Radcliffe and Hopkins moved against her. Got some evidence of rigged votes and fraud or somesuch crap."

"*What?*"

"*What?*"

Dani turned in surprise as both she and Danaar answered together. Isan had relaxed his grip on Shannon, letting go of her throat but keeping an arm around her waist. She rubbed at her neck as she looked from Dani to Danaar.

"Yeah. Packed her up and sent her off practically as soon as she got shipside. Never seen a political trial move so fast. They sent her to Mirax Ruas"

"Oh shit."

"What?" Danaar demanded, hand on Dani's arm

to swing her around. Sardaan growled, at her side in an instant, and Danaar lifted his hand.

"Don't worry." The big warrior lifted his hands, palms in the air. "I'm not after your female. I just want her to talk. What is this Mirax place?"

Dani nodded to Sardaan and he eased aside. She'd never get used to the sheer possessiveness Latharian males showed around their females. *Their females... he still considered her his.*

She put that thought aside for a second to focus on the big warrior in charge of the ship. War Commander Fenriis had left him in charge and the emperor seemed to consider him on the same level as Fenriis, so he had to be good at what he did.

"Mirax Ruas." Her voice was blunt and to the point for such a distasteful subject. "Maximum security. No guards. They throw the prisoners into the pit and make them mine *ferrianite* ore. It's a brutal place and not many survive it. Life expectancy is less than nine months, what with the manual labor, the conditions... and the other prisoners. It's a death sentence without having to order an execution."

She stopped talking as his face grew more and more thunderous. But it was nothing less than the truth. She'd heard prisoners who managed to survive the brutal conditions tattooed a band around their upper arms for each year they'd served. It was a simple ranking system that struck fear into the hearts of all who saw them on arriving at the prison. Only at the prison. No one ever left Mirax Ruas. Not alive anyway.

Danaar's expression set and for a moment she saw utter fury there. The kind of fury that would level entire worlds given half a chance.

"And they've sent Madison there?"

Dani half turned as Danaar motioned for Isan to let Shannon go. He did, begrudgingly, and she stepped forward, still rubbing at her neck.

"She was sent there a few days ago," she said, concern on her features. "It's why I disobeyed orders to try and rescue Da—Major General Black. She's the only other person who can confirm that the VP didn't give up secrets while she was aboard. The only other person they'll believe anyway."

Dani snorted in bitter amusement. "Yeah... not so much anymore. Not after I screwed up Radcliffe's stupid plans."

Shannon winced. "She's done for then. She'll never last in Ruas. She's a dead woman walking."

Danaar rumbled in the back of his throat,

reminding both women they were prisoners on an alien spacecraft.

"That's not your concern anymore," he told them shortly, nodding to the men behind them. "Sardaan, deal with your mate. Isan, make sure this prisoner gets to the cells."

Dani sucked a breath in, moving closer to Shannon. She opened her mouth to argue but didn't get the chance.

"No." Isan's voice was just as dangerous a growl as Danaar's had been.

"What?" The bigger warrior turned, his brow furrowed and anger on his face. "You dare defy me?"

Isan flicked his hair back over his shoulders, his expression just as forbidding. "I do. She's not going to the cells. She's coming with me. She's mine."

"I fucking well am not!" Shannon argued hotly, but both men ignored her.

Danaar nodded curtly. "Make sure she doesn't get into trouble. Dismissed, both of you."

"No! Leave her alone!" Dani struggled against Sardaan's hold as they were dragged off the bridge.

"Let me go, you asshole!" Shannon hissed, fighting Isan every step of the way. Like Sardaan, though, he was Lathar and easily kept the human woman under control. With a snarl, he threw her over one scarred shoulder and stalked off.

Dani turned on Sardaan, fear for her friend coloring her features. "Please, you have to help her," she begged, pressing her hands against his broad chest. He savored the feeling even though he knew it wasn't because she wished to touch him, but because she needed something from him. Still, she was actually looking at him now, not avoiding his gaze. He could work with that.

He covered her hands with his own, desperate to pull her into his arms again. All he wanted to do was hold her close without the stiffness or any barriers between them. But he didn't. Not yet. Softly, softly, he told himself.

"He won't hurt her," he told her gently, trying to reassure her. "I promise you that."

"How?" She looked worried, her hands still under his as she twisted to look toward the corridor Isan had carried the redheaded woman off down. "How can you promise that?"

He tucked a strong finger under her jaw and made her look at him. "Because he's looking at her like I looked at you when I first saw you. Because he's already halfway in love with her."

She froze, shock in her dark eyes for a moment. Then she shielded them with a downward sweep of her lashes and refused to look at him. "Don't say that." Her voice was as fragile and broken as he'd ever heard it, a soft whisper of sound he had to lean down to catch.

"Say what, *kelarris*?" He kept his voice low and soft, not wanting to scare her but also not prepared to let the subject slide. But even so, he was shocked to his core when he spotted the single tear tracking down her cheek.

"Don't say you loved me."

Guilt and shame hit him like a ship at max speed at her whispered words. The misery in her voice wrung out his heart and made him feel like the lowest of the low. A warrior without honor barely deserving the name. She was one of the strongest people he'd ever met, certainly stronger than a lot of warriors he knew, and he'd reduced her to tears.

"I won't," he murmured as he scooped her up into his arms and started to walk toward his quarters. They weren't far and this wasn't a conversation to be having in the corridors. He had too much to say to her, and he didn't want people listening in. She would be more comfortable in their own rooms.

"You won't?" Her voice was filled with confusion, but she didn't fight his hold on her, settling into the cradle of his arms easily. Her body betrayed her by relaxing marginally against his before she remembered to be wary of him and stiffened up a little. It was only a tiny movement, but it gave him hope that her defenses weren't completely raised against him.

"Nope."

He shook his head, hair dancing over his shoulders. She was watching him now, but he didn't look at her. Instead, he let her look her fill, only looking at her when he'd walked through the doors into their quarters and they'd closed behind him. Her look of confusion was adorable, but he easily caught the exhaustion and hurt lurking in the backs of her dark eyes.

"I won't say I loved you because that's not true," he clarified, turning and heading toward the seating area rather than the bed. He sank down into one of the low couches, settling her into his lap. She felt right curled up against his chest, her soft touch against his bare skin tormenting him.

"You don't? Then why didn't you leave me in the cells?" Her voice was a sharp gasp and she pushed against him, trying to get free of his arms. Whether it was a combination of exhaustion and misery, her struggles were no more than that of a week old *deearin* kit, easily contained.

"I won't say I *loved* you," he repeated, holding her still and stroking his thumb against the fullness of her lower lip. "Because that implies I no longer do. It's not that I loved you but that I *love* you."

She stilled, every movement frozen as she looked at him. Then she closed her eyes, shielding her expression from him again. Another tear leaked from the corner of her eye, from under the closed lid. Then another. And another.

"You Lathar," she whispered, shaking her head, her voice wavering. "You're so fucking literal."

She didn't open her eyes so he did the only thing he could think of. He leaned in to kiss her. Softly at first, brushing his lips over hers gently. He learned the shape of her lips again, not pushing her for more than she wanted to give. For a long moment she didn't move, just let him kiss her, and the tears streaming down her cheeks damn near broke his heart.

He pulled her closer, about to give up kissing her in favor of just holding her, and then it happened. Her fingers moved slightly against his chest. Just a small jerk at first, like she was just remembering how to move her hand after a long period of inactivity. At first he thought it was just a reflex, but then she touched him. Stroked his skin.

He caught his breath, lips stilling just against hers as he looked at her. She didn't open her eyes, even though he silently begged her to, but her lips softened under his. Slowly, watching for any sign she'd changed her mind, he pressed his lips against hers in the softest, gentlest kiss he could manage.

She didn't stiffen or push against him. Every cell in his body was hyperaware of hers, alert for any hint she was distressed or that his advances were unwelcome. But her lips were warm and soft, and her fingers stroked the skin over his chest gently. He didn't know if she was aware of the movement, but it drew a groan from the center of his chest and he kissed her again. He feathered his lips back and forth over hers.

"Please," he broke the kiss to whisper. "I didn't know you were being blackmailed. I swear."

She opened her eyes to look at him and he was met with the full force of her pain and misery. "But you thought the worst of me immediately. Didn't you? You didn't give me time or chance to explain. You were judge, jury and executioner, all rolled into one."

Guilt and shame welled up from his heart and soul and he closed his eyes.

"I did," he admitted. "I thought you'd betrayed us... *me*... and I was so angry I couldn't see anything else. Couldn't see beyond it or realize that you might have reasons for what you were doing."

"I did betray you," she whispered. "I hacked your system and let them onto your ship."

"You did." He smoothed her hair back from her

face, unable to stop touching her now he had her back in his arms. "But you had a reason."

She nodded. "I did what they ordered me to. Then I was going to come to you and tell you. But those bots found me first and..." She trailed off, darkness filling her eyes again. It didn't take a genius to work out the direction her thoughts had taken. The bots had taken her to the cells because he'd ordered them to.

"You told me everything," he said quietly, hand sliding into the nape of her neck as he watched her expression. "But it wasn't to save your own skin. Was it?"

She shook her head, closing her eyes against him again. Soft frustration filled him that she'd shielded herself from him, but he couldn't be angry with her. He'd figured it was her last line of defense and he wasn't going to take it from her. Not now.

"No. It was to stop Radcliffe and his team of idiots from making the biggest mistake in human history. We can't win a war against the Lathar. Ever."

"No, *kelarris*. You can't," he murmured, tilting her head to place a gentle kiss on her forehead. No wonder she'd risen as high as she had in the ranks of the human military. His mate was both beautiful and highly intelligent.

"It made me a traitor to my own people, telling you. I knew if they got me back I'd be going to Mirax Ruas too. But it didn't matter. I'd have saved you all. Stopped a war," she said softly, curled up against his chest. Silence fell for a few seconds. Then her next words made him freeze.

"Besides, I assumed you'd kill me anyway... so the threat of what Radcliffe would do to me didn't matter."

He closed his eyes again, shame and pain locking his body into place. His mate had assumed he, the male who had bonded to her, would... could *kill* her. And she'd given him the information anyway.

She'd saved her people thinking her life was already forfeited.

He groaned and pulled her closer, wanting to ease the misery in her voice. "I was mad at you, but I could never have hurt you, Dani. Ever." His words failed him for a moment, but then they tumbled out in a rush. A fall of words he couldn't control.

"I was so relieved that you talked. Told myself —*draanth,* I don't know what stupid shit I told myself—but I didn't have to do anything to get to you to talk and I wasn't going to argue. Because if you hadn't..." He pulled back to look into her eyes.

"I'd have been screwed. No matter how mad I was, how deep my fury, I could never hurt you. Ever."

Lifting his hand, holding it between them, he nodded toward his wrist. "Pull my cuff back."

She looked at him in confusion but then slowly reached out. With gentle fingers she pulled back the leather covering his wrist. Her frown deepened as she saw the dark marks winding around his skin.

"It looks like some kind of tattoo." Her gaze flicked to his, and he could tell she still had no idea what he was showing her. "I didn't think the Lathar did that. Tattoos, I mean?"

He shook his head. He'd heard about the human practice of injecting ink under the skin to decorate it and it sounded barbaric. "No. We don't have that kind of thing. Occasionally we might use *serranas* blood for tribal or honor markings but that's it."

He paused for a moment before continuing, watching her face carefully.

"They're not tattoos, Dani. They're mating marks."

HE HAD mating marks on his wrists. Dani had heard about the marks. They'd been mentioned in the small amount of information the Sentinel women had managed to get back to them.

"They are?"

He nodded, expression guarded as he simply watched her. Reaching out tentatively, she traced over the marks delicately with her fingertip. They weren't raised, and the skin was smooth. Like the design was etched underneath.

"They're..." She looked at him steadily. "Mating marks for you, the Lathar, are like marriage. More so than just claiming a woman, right?"

He nodded again, a small sound of pleasure in the back of his throat as she continued touching him.

"It's everything. Once a female calls mating marks in a male's skin, that's it for him. For as long as I live, you are my everything." His arm tightened around her waist. "I'll never love another, for as long as I draw breath. But I didn't need marks to tell me that, Dani. I've loved you since the moment I saw you on that view screen. I knew then you were meant to be mine."

She gave a small smile, the little kernel of hope that had been growing since he'd taken the gun off her in the cells blossoming. "That would have been kind of difficult given we were on different ships."

He pulled her closer, his marked hand cupping the side of her neck. "I would have found a way. Taken on your entire fleet, singlehandedly, for the chance to win your heart. For a chance that you might, one day, love me back."

His gaze searched hers and she saw the desperation and conflict hidden in his soul. "Please tell me I haven't ruined any chance for us. That I haven't made you hate me with what I did..."

Her heart melted, the last little resistance she had against him gone with the need and misery in his deep voice.

She shook her head, her voice soft as she answered. "No, I don't hate you. I couldn't... ever hate you. How can you hate someone you love?"

His grip tightened on the back of her neck and he closed his eyes for a second, his expression tight with relief.

"Thank the goddess," he breathed and pulled her closer to plunder her lips. The kiss was long and drugging, filled with emotion and need. She sighed, the sound lost in his mouth, and wrapped her arms around his broad shoulders to kiss him back.

Although the kiss started off soft, it didn't stay that way for long. His tongue parted her lips in a soft sweep, and he slid deep inside with a groan, teasing and caressing hers with long, slow strokes. Heat exploded through her, the need to touch him overwhelming all else. With a moan of frustration, she pulled at his leather jacket, needing to touch his skin.

He lifted her up and within minutes, their clothing was gone; pulled off by him, or her, or both of them... she didn't know which and didn't care. All that mattered was getting more of his kisses, touching more of his body. Having him touch her.

Barely breaking their kiss, she lay back on the large couch, the leather cool at her back. He was braced over her, his weight on his forearms as he slid an arm under her neck to pillow her head. His hair-roughened knee parted hers and he settled between her thighs, the heavy weight of his erection pressed against her pussy lips.

"Dani... *kelarris*," he broke the kiss long enough to whisper against her lips. "Are you sure about this? We can wait—"

She cut him off with a hard kiss, plundering his mouth with ravenous slides and strokes of her tongue. They were both breathless when she pulled away to look up into his eyes.

"I'm sure," she whispered. "I need this. I need

you. Please, Sardaan... I love you. Make all the bad memories between us right."

He smiled and leaned down to steal the softest kiss she could recall him giving her. It was innocent and sweet in its purity. A promise of love and happiness to last a lifetime.

Then he moved, his cock pressing against the entrance to her body, and he slid into her in one smooth, long movement. She moaned against his lips as he bottomed out, her pussy fluttering and clenching hard around him.

"Oh gods," he groaned, gathering her close to him as he pulled back to gaze into her eyes.

Slowly, he began to move, his hips pumping in a slow, sensuous rhythm against hers. Each slow pull back and slide seated him deeply within her, his thick cock stroking nerve endings that then cascaded pleasure through her entire body.

But the physical pleasure was secondary to the look on his face as he moved over her, their locked gazes allowing her to see how every little movement affected him. Allowed her to see the love in his eyes as he made them one. She wrapped her arms around him, moving with him, each rock of her hips welcoming him. Cradling him.

But all too soon the emotional needs gave way to

the carnal. His face tightened, his thrusts speeding up. Bracing himself over her, a fine sheen of sweat covered his chest and shoulders as he powered into her. His hair swung against his shoulders, the cords in his neck standing out as he drove them both closer to pleasure.

She arched her back, closing her eyes as she chased that edge with him. They moved together in perfect concert. A true partnership, as equals. That thought, the love in his eyes as he looked at her, the feeling of his thick cock buried deeply inside her, all conspired against her and she cried out as her body tightened.

"Oh god... Sardaan, *please...*" she moaned, clinging to him as he sped up.

"I got you, *kelarris*," he promised, voice rough with passion. "Let go. I'll catch you. I'll always catch you."

So she did. Her body clenched hard around his as she came in long, hard waves of pleasure. It crashed through her, like a sensual barrage, tumbling over and through her like a thousand shards of glass bouncing and cascading off each other. Hard-edged and all consuming, it left her gasping for breath and holding on to him. He was her anchor, her support, everything she needed.

"Holy *draanth*," he hissed, his moan guttural as her body tightened around his cock, milking him in hard waves. He slammed into her. Harder. Faster. Movements jerkier, not as smooth as they were before. Then, he threw his head back and bellowed, thrusting into her one last time as he came. Hard and fast.

She whimpered as she felt him explode deep within her, his hot seed bathing her inner walls. It felt like he was filling her up and she bit her lip, hoping that maybe his seed would find fertile ground. Was a baby between them even possible? Just the thought made her wrap herself around him, her heart soft and giving as she whispered into his ear. "I love you, Sardaan K'Vass. I always have."

He paused to smooth her hair back from her face, his expression serious as he looked down at her.

"I love you too, Danielle K'Vass. I promise you'll never regret forgiving me. And I'll prove it to you every day for the rest of our lives."

EPILOGUE

"*S*eriously?" The young *Quesen's* eyes flickered from Dani to Sardaan and back again, confusion evident on his features. "You want me to hit a *female?* What if I hurt her? Females are delicate."

Dani snorted, her lips quirking with amusement as her husband, elevated to centurion and now in charge of *Quesen* training, just smiled and spread his hands.

"Hit her or don't hit her because she sure as *draanth* is going to hit you. *Listen up,*" he lifted his voice so the eager crowd of youngsters around them could hear him. "Humans are smaller and faster than we are, and you could learn a lot from them.

UP TO AND INCLUDING how to beat a much bigger warrior. It's happened. Just ask Konaat T'Kiis."

Dani's lips quirked. The story of her defeat of Konaat had become legend, the warrior disappearing from court as far as she'd heard. She settled into a guard position to watch as the *Quesen* circled her, his expression intent. She had no idea what the future would hold for her, but she knew one thing for sure.

It would be here, with the man she loved.

Her sexy alien husband. Her bonded mate.

Thank you for reading **BONDED TO THE ALIEN CENTURION.** I hope you enjoyed it!

The next book in the Warriors of the Lathar series is **HITCHED TO THE ALIEN GENERAL!**

Her perfect man is a big, scarred alien war hero. Pity he only see's her as a warrior, not a woman...

Kenna Reynolds loves life in the Imperial Court. The

latharian culture fascinates her, and she values the friendships she's made amongst the sentinel women, most bonded to Latharian males, and a few with babies on the way. She wants that, but the male she wants—Xaandril, the emperor's champion—barely seems to notice her as a woman. As a warrior yes, but she's begun to lose all hope that he'll ever see her as a woman...

She was his the moment he saw her. But how can he claim her when he's less than half a warrior?

After losing his family years ago Xaandril, the emperor's champion, never thought he'd find love again. When the first humans are discovered to be compatible, Xaan decides to leave finding a mate among them to younger males. But one of the humans, Kenna, won't give up on him, not even when he's grievously inured in battle.
It takes seeing her dancing with another warrior to get his ass into gear, but before he can claim her unusual readings in a far flung terran system have them heading on on a mission for the Emperor himself.

What they find is a disturbing debris field, a colony

with more secrets than members and a hidden enemy. Can Xaan beat them all to save the woman he loves, or will he lose everything, including his heart, once again?

GET YOUR COPY NOW!

(minacarter.com/book/hitched-to-the-alien-general)

ABOUT THE AUTHOR

Mina Carter is a *New York Times & USA Today* bestselling author of romance in many genres. She lives in the UK with her husband, daughter, a tank of a Staffordshire Bull Terrier, and a bossy cat.

Connect with Mina online at:
minacarter.com

I appreciate your help in spreading the word, including telling friends. Reviews help readers find new books! Please leave a review on your favorite book site!

SIGN UP TO MY NEWSLETTER!
https://minacarter.com/newsletter/

facebook.com/minacarterauthor
instagram.com/minacarter77
bookbub.com/profile/mina-carter

Printed in Great Britain
by Amazon

30418972R00141